The Legend of
Link Bonner

Link Bonner never wanted to gain a reputation as a fast hand with a six-gun and the will to use it. But sometimes circumstances drive the lives of men even beyond their own desires. Bonner was such a man, always in the middle of trouble he was not looking for.

It took a woman to change Bonner and losing her made life and death of little consequence to him. But the man he was also changed the West for the better. Without his kind, many more innocent people would have died. To the end he fought for what he thought right, down to the last bullet.

By the same author

Blood Red Star

Writing as Art Isberg
Showdown in Badlands
Will Keen, Indian Scout

The Legend of Link Bonner

Shorty Gunn

A Black Horse Western

ROBERT HALE

© Shorty Gunn 2018
First published in Great Britain 2018

ISBN 978-0-7198-2706-8

The Crowood Press
The Stable Block
Crowood Lane
Ramsbury
Marlborough
Wiltshire SN8 2HR

www.bhwesterns.com

Robert Hale is an imprint
of The Crowood Press

The right of Shorty Gunn to be identified as
author of this work has been asserted by him
in accordance with the Copyright, Designs and
Patents Act 1988

Typeset by
Derek Doyle & Associates, Shaw Heath
Printed and bound in Great Britain by
4Bind Ltd, Stevenage, SG1 2XT

*To my wife, Ruth Dolores, who has always shown me the right
road to follow*

CHAPTER ONE

An icy, blustering wind swept grey storm-clouds with dark bellies racing over jagged mountain peaks. The bleak setting made it a perfect day for a funeral. The gravesite on a rocky hill-top, devoid of anything taller than weeds, played host to only a dozen people bundled against the wind, none of which could rightly be called mourners. Everyone had a different opinion and story to tell about the life and times of the man lying in the plain pine coffin. Some only wanted to be able to say they'd actually attended the burial. Others were openly glad he was gone. A few had brief encounters with Bonner when he was alive and wild stories had sprung from them.

Because Link Bonner was not a man of God, no sober-faced, black-frocked pastor or reverend in town would lead the burial to read over his departed soul, if he had one. Instead, one big man with a mat of grey hair, beard and mustache to match, stood at the head of the gathering, holding his wide-brimmed hat in one hand. James 'Bull' Tate pulled the back of his hand across his mouth, trying to come up with the proper words to say good-bye. In his younger days, the big, raw-boned man had been a

7

working cowboy and once even did a stint at wearing a lawman's badge. He garnered the moniker 'Bull' boasting he could ride a longhorn bull for ten full seconds for ten-dollars, and often did. Now he was old, grey and bent from the rough life and times he'd lived through. He was the only person at the gathering who really knew Bonner on a close, personal basis from the times they'd spent together as young men. He cleared his throat with a cough over the whistling wind before starting to speak.

'I've lived long enough to know sometimes a man does things not everyone else agrees with or even understands. This man here, Link Bonner, was that kind of man. Back when all this country around here was wild and wide open, every man was his own law by the kind of iron he carried on his hip. You might have to make a split-second decision to pull it over some kind of dispute, or never live long enough to make another one. It wasn't like today with your quiet streets, full-time sheriff, churches, schoolhouse and ranches scattered all over the country. But I'll tell all of you this. I'm certain if it wasn't for a man like Link, none of this would be here today. The Old West needed a man like him whether you agree with how he lived it or not. Everyone in Mountain Gate owes him that. Now I've said about all I'm going to say except . . . lower the box.'

The small gathering shuffled slowly back to their horses and buggies, making their way downhill, while Tate stood alone a moment longer before nodding at the pair of grave diggers to begin filling the hole. As dirt and rocks echoed off the wooden coffin, he wondered if all those years had been worth ending up like this. Maybe, he thought, some of what he'd said might sink in to the minds of those attending the funeral even though they could not know what the world he and Link lived through

THE LEGEND OF LINK BONNER

was really like.

After riding back into Mountain Gate, Tate walked into the High Timber saloon, taking up residence at his usual table over in one corner near the Faro table. He sat glumly, shoving back thick, grey hair from his face before unbuttoning his heavy jacket. Easing back in the chair with a grunt of despair, he thought about his old friend, slowly being buried under the cold, rocky ground. If there was one thing he was sure of, it was that life in town and the rest of the west would never be the same again. All the old timers were going or had already gone. Bonner was the biggest name of them all. He stood for a time when men really were men and backed it up with a six-gun. It was a time before shining steel rails and black-smoking locomotives invaded the solitude of the west, and every town had a law-man wearing a tin star, even locking up some drunk that couldn't hold his liquor. That past time was a way of life both Indian and white man fought to preserve and keep each in their own way. Tate wondered if both had lost that battle.

Two men got up from the Faro table, walking over to Tate's. Pulling out chairs, they slowly sat down, never taking their eyes off the old cowboy. Several more at the bar saw he was obviously unhappy, joining them until a circle surrounded Bull. One man finally spoke up, daring to reach over, putting a hand on Tate's shoulder for support.

'We all know you're feeling down over Link's death. Everyone knows you two were close back in the old days. Can talking about it help any? We'd sure like to hear it.'

Tate pulled at his whiskers, eyeing the men around him, wondering if it was even worth the effort. What could any of them know or understand of that world, before they were even born, in town, in a soft feather bed and warm house. He stared back without answering.

'Hey, Dink,' one man shouted to the counter-man. 'Pass a new bottle over here and a clean glass too. It's on me. We want to hear what Bull has to say. He needs a little tongue oil to start up!'

Dink Hall handed a bottle of Old Manor and glass with it, over the bar top. 'You sure you can afford the whole bottle?' he questioned while chewing on the stump of a cigar.

'Of course I'm sure. Besides, it's for a good reason. Bull knows all there is to know about Link Bonner and how things used to be around here.' He pulled the bottle top off, pouring a stubby glass full with amber-colored liquid. 'Go ahead, Bull, we're all listening. What was it really like in the old days?'

Bull eyed the men, expectantly leaning forward waiting to catch every word. He took in a slow breath. If they were all so fired up to hear about it, why didn't any of them attend the burial, he wondered. Then he remembered not a single clergyman did either. The anger of their slur slowly passed when he realized he was the only man left to speak up for his old friend. He reached over, lifting the shot glass, eyeing it while thinking there must be a thousand memories in the rest of that bottle. Maybe just a few would be enough to satisfy everyone, telling stories they all wanted to hear. Tate lifted the glass higher, taking it down in one quick hook.

'I guess it all started for me and Link back in the forties. We were down near Indian Territory, just two young cowboys ripping and running wherever the wind took us. We both got jobs working for Arlee Cox's cattle outfit. He was building up a big herd of longhorns and needed

10

drovers to handle them all. Rustlers were bold and wild back then, cutting out dozens of head if they could get away with it. Cox made it clear to both of us if we caught anyone, we were to try to stop them, and didn't much care how we did it. It was plain he meant six-guns if it came to that. He said when he had enough beef, he meant to drive them all the way north to Abilene, Kansas. There was talk of building a railroad up there and he wanted to be first with his beef. That was even before Jesse Chisholm marked out the trail some years later that became so famous for other cattle drives. Me and Link were out riding nighthawk. . . .'

'What's nighthawk?' one man questioned.

'Big cattle outfits kept men out on their stock both day and night. Nighttime was when most trouble could happen. Lighting storms and thunder could spook the cattle into a running stampede. You had to try and stop them anyway you could. Sometimes you couldn't, and they'd be scattered all over the country the next day with some dead from being trampled by the others. Wolves and mountain lions also did most of their killing at night when they could move in close. The worst of it was two-legged wolves, though. Rustlers could be real big trouble.'

'You ever run into any of them?' a listener broke in.

'Yeah, that's what I'm getting to. Me and Link were riding nighthawk when I heard him whistle to me. I rode over to see what he wanted. . .' Bull began to reminisce.

'I heard some longhorns making a ruckus on the edge of the herd,' Link said. 'We better ride over that way and see if there's anything to it. The glow off this half moon will give us at least a little light.'

When they got close he motioned for both of them to get down and lead their horses. There were still some

11

cattle in front of them when they just made out four or five riders trying to cut out some animals. Both groups saw each other about the same time and all hell broke loose. One of them opened fire. Bull ducked down but Link started running toward them, firing back, just as the long-horns cut loose, starting to run. Tate heard one of the rustlers yell out, then it was all lost to the sound of hoofs thundering across the ground in a stampede.

'Mount up or we'll end up ground into dust!' Link yelled, both men leaping into their saddles, riding reck-lessly after the wild-running cattle, out into the night. It took a five-mile run plus other men from the main camp to finally get ahead of the herd and turn and slow them down, finally stopping the bawling and jostling mass of animals. Arlee Cox was one of those men.

'Who was riding nighthawk?' Cox asked.

'I think it was Bonner and Tate,' one of the cowboys said.

'Anyone seen them?'

'No,' another answered. 'But you can't see much of any-thing in this dark either.'

'All right, just keep the cattle together and don't let them break out again. They're still moving and jittery. It won't take much for them to cut loose again. I'll find Tate and Bonner on my own.'

Cox rode around to the far side of the herd where he found the two men. 'Is that you, Link?' he called out.

'Yeah. We had one hell of a ride, didn't we!'

'Worse than that, I could have lost some animals getting run over too. You two were on watch. What started it?'

'Rustlers,' Bull broke in. 'They opened up on me and Link when we rode in on them.'

'Opened up? Link, is that your story too?'

12

'I heard the cattle sounding nervous and took Bull with me to ride over and see what was going on. When we got close, we could make out four or five men trying to cut out some animals. The second they saw us, one of them started shooting. That spooked the cattle into a run.'

'Did you fire back?'

'You bet I did. I wasn't going to stand there and get shot down. I heard one of them cry out. I must have got a bullet in him.'

Arlee didn't comment for several long moments, thinking all this over. When he did, the sound in his voice made it clear he was deeply worried about what Link told him.

'That's all I need. Rustlers and now a shooting on top of it.'

'I didn't have any selection in it,' Link responded. 'You told us when we hired on, to stop anyone trying to rustle your stock. That's what we did. Twenty-dollars a month pay isn't worth getting killed over.'

'All right. I guess I can see that too. When it gets light enough we'll ride back where all this started and see if we can find someone or if they rode off with the other men. The rest of my men can handle the herd now.'

A gloomy dawn lit the sky behind scattered bands of dark clouds from the storm that passed off to the north. The three men rode tracing the direction back, following chewed-up ground left by running longhorns. As light grew, the trail became easier.

'We should be close,' Cox reined his horse to a halt. 'Let's spread out and move real slow. This looks like about where the cattle started running.'

The riders fanned out, only going a short distance before Bull called out, 'Over here. Looks like you put someone on the ground for sure, Link!' He waved his hat

13

over his head.

The men converged on Tate, stepping down surrounding the body of a man crumpled at a grotesque angle. 'Would you look at that,' Bull's voice was low, in awe. 'He's nearly been stomped to pieces.'

Cox knelt, slowly rolling over the broken body, leaning closer. 'I don't believe it,' he whispered.

'Don't believe what?' Link questioned. 'You know who this is?'

'Unfortunately, I do. This is Burl Teague's son, Rory, or what's left of him. There's going to be big trouble over this for all of us, and especially you, Link. I don't think this kid was much over sixteen years old.'

'He was old enough to pull a trigger.'

'Yes, I understand that, but Teague won't. I knew the kid had a wild streak, but never thought he'd go this far. I'll have to take him home.'

'Remember, he had help too,' Bull added. 'There's other riders who know what went on here, and it's not Link's fault it happened.'

'If you want, I'll ride over with you and tell this Teague how it happened. There's no reason for you to take the heat by yourself.'

'No, that's something I don't want you to do. The old man would probably draw down on you the second he heard you killed his kid. It's something I'll have to do on my own. I don't want anyone else getting shot down. If you two went with me, Teague might think we came for another fight. Get me a blanket and we'll wrap him up. Bull, ride back double fast to the ranch and get me a pack horse.'

'You ought to let me go with you even if Bull stays here,' Link tried again.

14

'I said no, Link, and that's final. I know Teague. You don't. This is going to go down hard enough as it is. I don't want you anywhere near Teague or his men. Bull, get going.'

'If you won't let me go with you, at least let Bull and I ride as far as the Big Muddy. We can wait for you there while you cross over, until you get back. There's no sense in you being out there alone after what you're going to deliver.'

The sun was already reaching toward mid-day when the riders reached the banks of the river. Even though the overnight storm had passed to the north, the sudden downpour had swollen the normally wide, shallow water-way into a sloshing current of brown, muddy waves rushing by.

'You sure you can cross here?' Bull questioned as all three men eyed the hissing river. 'Pulling that pack horse too, could be a handful.'

'I should be able to,' Cox nodded. 'It's wide but this is still the shallowest place to cross.'

'Maybe Bull and I should at least stay with you until you reach the other side?' Link suggested.

'No, you two stay here. I'll be back in about an hour or maybe a little more. Teague's ranch is not too far on the other side through those low buttes over there. The sooner I get this done the better. I'll see you then. Wait for me right here.'

Cox spurred his already-nervous horse into the current, pulling the pack horse behind him with Rory Teague's body roped on, as Link and Bull sat in the saddle watching him. Half-way across, the fast-moving water already came up to both horses' bellies as they fought to keep their feet against the powerful current. Suddenly, the packer lost his footing, going down in icy water up to its neck, struggling frantically, twisting and turning trying to regain its feet. The blanket-wrapped body broke loose, rolling over and over as the current began washing it fast downstream. Cox yanked his horse around after it.

'Come on!' Link shouted, spurring his horse down the gravelly bank at full gallop with Bull right behind him. In seconds, they came even with the bobbing body and Link raced his horse into the river at full stride, forcing the powerful animal to swim closer. He untied his lariat, swinging it in a widening arc over his head before a long toss splashed in, curling the rope under the corpse, the current cinching it tight. Link quickly took in the slack, until pulling the blanket-wrapped body over the saddle in front of him, swimming his horse for the far shore.

Arriving there, Arlee and Bull bailed off their horses, taking the soaking-wet body of Rory Teague down from Link's grip. 'Well, this ought to do it if nothing else will.' The boss man's breath came in short gasps from the dangerous dunking he'd just taken. 'Not only do I have to bring the kid back to his father, but bring him back like this.'

'Will you let me and Bull ride in with you now?' Link tried one more time. 'You're going to need all the help you can get, aren't you?'

Cox hesitated a moment, rubbing the back of his neck, kicking the gravelly ground with his boot, struggling for an answer. 'No, I just don't think that will work. I want you two to ride back to the other side and wait for me. I'll get out of this, one way or the other. It's still better I go in there alone, not with any guns backing me up. I'll get back here soon as I can.'

Bonner and Bull helped retie the body on the packer

before watching Cox ride away. 'I hope he knows what he's doing.' Tate wondered out loud.

'He better. He called it. Now he'll have to play out his hand without any help from us. I don't know who this Teague is, but he'd been better off with us backing him like I said. All we can do is get back across the Muddy and wait for him over there, if he comes back at all.'

Once on the far shore, both men waited as the afternoon sun slowly burned its way across the sky. The horses stood still, heads down, while the pair marked time walking up and down the gravelly bank with Bull occasionally tossing a flat rock into the water to see how far it would skip. Link sat on a log, washed up on shore, staring across the river, saying little. Half an hour passed then a second one. Bull walked over, bored and restless, sitting down next to him.

'What's taking him so darn long anyway? He said Teague's place was just past those buttes over there.'

'I imagine there's a lot being said.'

'Yeah, and I'll bet most of it has your name on it too, after killing that kid.'

'Maybe, but he had it coming. I won't hear any argument about that.'

'You moved so fast I didn't know what was going on for a moment.'

'Moving slow can get you killed. Anyone who wants to strap on a six-gun better be ready to use it whether he's fifteen or fifty. If they don't, they should take up farming, plowing behind a mule.'

Over the noise of their conversation and the rushing water, Bonner suddenly came to his feet, still staring hard across the Muddy. 'You hear that?' he asked.

Tate came to his feet, cupping one hand behind his ear.

Now he got it too. 'Sounds like shooting way off. I'm pretty sure it is.'

Link stepped to his horse, yanking his rifle out of its scabbard. Bull did the same thing. 'You think we should swim the horses back over there? Cox could be in some kind of trouble.'

'No, if it's him and he can reach the river, anyone after him will have to try crossing too. That makes them slow, easy targets. First he has to get over here on his own.'

The two men stood watching the far bank, tall with brush as the sound of shooting grew closer, until a lone rider broke out of cover, charging his horse into the water, throwing up big fans of spray.

'That's Cox!' Tate shouted.

The boss man was a third of the way across the Muddy when three more riders burst through the willows into the water, firing wildly at the fleeing cattleman. Geysers of water erupted around Cox and his horse while he clung low in the saddle, urging the animal further out into the strong current.

'Let 'em have it!' Bonner ordered, both men opening-up with rifle fire.

One of Teague's cowboy's horses reared up, whinnying in pain, throwing the rider off into the current, out of action. His two pals kept coming, one firing at Cox, the other beginning to shoot back at Link and Tate. Bonner concentrated his fire on that man until he screamed in pain, falling off into the river, trying to stay afloat and swim with his one arm. His *amigo* had enough, yanking his horse around trying to get back to the shore before he was hit too. Arlee finally reached the bank, kicking his horse onto dry ground, before looking back as his pursuers.

'Let's get out of here before anyone else shows up to

help them!' he ordered.

'I said you should have taken us with you, remember?' Link had to say it as he and Bull pulled themselves up into their saddles. 'If you did, they might not have tried to bushwhack you!'

'No time to talk about that now. Let's ride!'

CHAPTER TWO

Arlee Cox paced back and forth on the front porch of his ranch house, with trouble on his mind. His deeply-furrowed brow showed that, even before he spoke a word. His thirteen cowboys stood by the hitching-rail looking up waiting for him to speak. They already pretty well knew why he'd called them there. He stopped his pacing, turning to grip the handrail with both hands, eyeing his men.

'I don't have to tell you men we could have a range war brewing. Some of Burl Teague's men tried to rustle my stock. Link and Bull stopped them, but it took a killing to do so. Young Rory Teague was the one who got shot. I tried to reason with Teague, but he wouldn't have any of it. I want all of you to know right now what could be coming because of it. I know you only signed on with me to work longhorns, but with things the way they are, it could take more than a lariat and a fast horse. Six-guns are now in the mix. Anybody don't want to face that, speak up right now. I'll tell all of you straight up I don't blame any man who doesn't. You might not only get yourself shot but someone working alongside you too.'

One of the younger cowhands, Paul Tyler, raised his

hand hesitantly. Cox nodded for him to speak. 'I've only been married a year and my wife's got our first child about to pop. I'd like to stay on, but I'd also like to be around to see my child grow up. I guess I have to go. I'm sorry, Arlee.'

'That's all right, Paul. I understand, believe me I do. You've been a good hand, but don't take that chance. Your family is a lot more important now than a bunch of ornery, fly-infested longhorns. See my daughter, Alberta, and she'll get your pay. Anyone else?'

An older man with snow-white sideburns, raised his hand, stepping forward pushing his hat back on his head. 'I might have stuck here when I was a younger man, but I'm no gunfighter either. I'd likely end up in a pine box, if I tried. I think it's best I pull out too, much as I hate to. Ain't too many outfits will hire a man my age. You've been an all right boss, but my old woman would be lost without me, so I'll have to go look for something else, if I can find it.'

'You do what you have to, Tex. Maybe if things cool down you can come back.'

Cox looked across the faces of the remaining men as the two who quit headed for the bunk-house to pick up personal belongings.

'Is that all of it?' he questioned. 'OK, the rest of you want to stick with me I appreciate it. Now there's one more thing I have to say, and I want all of you to be aware of it. Be careful about going into town unless you have to for some reason. If you do, do it in pairs. Teague's men already tried to come after me. They might try anything in there too.'

'I'm not staying out of Mesquite because of Teague or anyone else,' Link spoke up, the rest of the men turning toward him. 'We've got as much right to be there as

21

anyone else. No one is going to bull dog me over what happened.'

'I'm with Link,' Bull spoke up. 'We'll go where we want. So should anyone else here. They've got a lawman in town, don't they? His job is to keep trouble down.'

'He's not much of a sheriff.' Cox shook his head. 'He's Teague's cousin. He's got him in his back pocket. Don't expect any kind of help if it comes to that. Remember what I said, all of you. Now let's get back to work and be careful. Keep your eyes open day and night, too.'

Mesquite really wasn't much of a town, situated out on a dusty, cactus-dotted plain. No timber boom or gold and silver strike shouted out its name to lure men in from both near and far, with dreams of sudden riches. Instead it was first an old Indian encampment used by the Wichitas and Apaches traveling through that part of the country before white cattlemen moved into the area years later. The dirt main street became a muddy quagmire when rains poured down in winter, then baked hard as bricks when summer sun fired the land in sizzling heat. The sketchy buildings lining the street were both board and flat-topped mixed adobe. At one end of town a small church had been built by those endeavoring to pave their way out of Mesquite into heaven. No school house was constructed but four saloons went up quickly, along with a feed store, dry goods store, tack shop, blacksmith's shop, a small livery stable and sheriff's office. The other buildings lining the street were occupied by men selling everything from firearms, to clothes and boots, plus building lots, both in and out of town, if a land rush ever came, unlikely as that was. Two small eateries were also in business, one serving Mexican food, the other a Chinese restaurant, for those more adventurous.

Burl Teague's cousin, Austin Waite, walked the sidewalks of town, dispensing his own brand of justice, kept in office by his powerful relative. There was no election for sheriff. Teague appointed him, and he stayed appointed. No one would run against him for fear they might end up missing or dead. Only Arlee Cox had sometimes challenged the dominance of both Teague and Waite, because of occasional flare-ups between the two cattlemen. Rory Teague's death had changed everything into an even deadlier situation. Teague swore he'd either run Cox out of the cattle business, or see him dead and buried in the town's weed-choked cemetery. He wasn't a man to ignore. He'd given Waite orders to run Arlee's men out of town if they showed up, or put them in jail if they didn't move out. The fuse was lit, burning quickly toward a powder keg of real trouble. Link Bonner would help fan those flames even faster.

Ten days after the attempted ambush of Cox on the Muddy, Link and Bull rode into town to pick up supplies Arlee had ordered for the ranch. The two were the only ones who volunteered for the job. The other cowboys were content to let them. They'd stuck their necks out staying with Cox as promised. They wouldn't stick them out that far in a town controlled by Burl Teague. Bonner took the job as much to help out Cox, as show he wasn't going to let anyone tell him where he could and couldn't go. Bull went along to back him up as he always did. They took a wagon instead of their horses.

In the alley behind Charles Good's tack shop and leather goods, Good lifted the last heavy box into the back of the wagon before mopping his perspiring brow. 'That does it. Come inside and I'll figure up the bill,' he invited.

The three men went inside, up to the counter where

Good wet a pencil with his tongue and began figuring a column of numbers for the total. Just as he reached the bottom, a sudden commotion and shouting outside on the street got the three men's attention. Bull walked to the window, looking out as Bonner eyed him for an explanation.

'Hey, that looks like that young cowboy Paul Tyler, used to work for Cox. C'mere quick, Link.'

Bonner crossed the room, looking outside. Three of Teague's cowboys were beating up Tyler, repeatedly knocking him down every time he tried to get up, while his pregnant wife stood up in their wagon, crying, screaming for them to stop.

'Come on!' Link shouted, rushing to the door, shoving it open. Outside, twenty feet away, the trio were still enjoying themselves. They turned at his shout.

'You thugs pretty sure of yourselves three on one. Let's see what you can do when the odds are closer.'

Bonner and Bull stood side by side, hands dropping inches from six-guns. The Teague boys glanced at each other, surprised at the unexpected challenge. For one spine-tingling moment, no one moved until Link spoke again, steady, cool, demanding.

'Kid, you get up in the wagon out of the way. You three bums pick up those packages you scattered all over the street. Put them back in the wagon and get out of here while you can.'

'Mister, who do you think you are? You're messing with Teague cowboys. You go to hell!' One of the men snarled, stabbing a hand for his pistol.

Bonner's six-gun cleared leather, spitting fire and hot lead, Bull matching him. The back-talker twisted to the ground with a groan along with a second cowboy next to him. The last man quickly threw up his hands, terrified, shouting at the top of his lungs not to shoot. Link stepped up face to face, his pistol pressing against the cowboy's belt-buckle. Lifting the man's pistol out of its holster, he tossed it out into the street as a throng of men rushed out of saloons and stores to see what the sudden shooting was all about. Link wasn't done with the last Teague cowboy just yet.

'I said you pick up those packages. I won't tell you again.'

The petrified man knelt, gathering up the bundles, placing them back in Tyler's wagon, never taking his eyes off Bonner as he did so.

'Now you get on your horse and get out of here,' Link ordered. 'And you can tell your boss if he tries something like this again, he'll be facing me next time, not his help.'

Sheriff Austin Waite pushed his way through the crowd of men up to the bodies of the two men lying in the dirt. His eyes instantly fell on Bonner.

'You have a hand in this?' he asked, sizing up the stranger.

'I did. These two and their pal were beating up the young man in that wagon, terrifying his pregnant wife. I told them to stop. They decided to pull on me instead. It was a big mistake.'

Waite eyed Bonner warily before turning to the men surrounding them. 'Any of you see what happened here, speak up?'

'He's telling the truth.' Tyler's wife Loretta suddenly stood from the wagon as Paul came up beside her, wiping the blood from his mouth. 'Those men were beating up my husband for no reason at all. We don't know them, and they didn't know us.' She began sobbing again.

'Anyone else?' Waite's mouth pulled tight with displeasure at her answer.

'That's how it was, sheriff,' young Tyler answered. 'They said they were beating on me because I used to work for Arlee Cox's outfit, even though I don't anymore. If it wasn't for Link and Bull here, that might be me on the ground dead instead of those two men.'

Waite turned back to Bonner. 'I'll have to take your pistol and your friend's too, until I get more of this story figured out. You'll have to come with me.'

'You're not taking anything from either of us, and we're not going anywhere,' Link was fast to answer. 'You can tell your cousin if he orders something like this again, he's going to wish he hadn't. I may even tell him myself one of these days.'

The crowd suddenly became deathly quiet at Link's bold refusal, beginning to step back, away from the three men in case more gunplay was about to explode. Waite's breath quickened as a tremor of fear shot through him. No one had ever questioned anything he'd ordered before because of who backed him. Now he felt alone, stripped bare of power, facing a man who clearly had no intention of being told what to do, by him or anyone else. Finally, he summoned enough courage to answer.

'You and the rest of the men out at Cox's ranch aren't welcome here in Mesquite. You can tell Cox that too. If you're smart, you'll stay out of town before you start a range war you can't win. Better remember what I said.'

'It's already started, and Teague is the one who started it. We'll come into town anytime we want. Don't you try to stop us, or you'll regret it. You're as crooked as a dog's hind leg, and everyone here knows it. Save your orders for someone else. They don't mean anything to me or the other men working for Cox.'

Waite's face turned pasty-white. He didn't dare push it any further, facing someone who'd just shot down two of his friends, and looked ready to do it again. Very slowly he began backing up, never taking his eyes off Bonner until swallowed up by the crowd snickering with subdued laughter.

Doyle Brand stood hat in hand, wide-eyed in fear in front of Burl Teague, spilling out the story of what happened in town and the killing of his two pals by Link Bonner. When he finished, Teague's eyes narrowed, and his face twisted in rage.

'What were you doing standing there while this Bonner and his friend shot down Hoyt and Jo-ell!' Burl shouted at the top of his lungs, spittle flying from his lips. 'You ought to be dead on the ground along with them. Instead, you come back here like a sniveling school boy with some cock and bull story about a gunman with a fast hand!'

'I tell you he was too quick to pull on. I never even got my pistol out of its holster before the shooting was over. Him and the other big man have to be professional gun-slingers to move like that. Ain't no cowboy going to out-pull him. Cox must have hired him special for it.'

Teague turned away with a grunt of disgust, tossing the glass of whiskey he was holding into the big, stone fireplace, shattering it, as his mind raced. Without turning back, he began forming a plan, speaking slowly in a low, menacing voice.

'So . . . Cox went and hired himself a gun-hand, huh . . . well two can play that game.' He turned back to Brand. 'Go back out with the longhorns. You're no good for anything else. When you get there, tell Alviso Luna I want to see him in here and fast. Now get out of my sight!'

An hour later, Luna stood before Teague. Taking off his big, Mexican sombrero in respect for his gringo boss, he wondered why he'd been called into the spacious, private office for the first time.

'You know the name Jack Buck?' Teague questioned.

'*Sí*, I know of him,' Luna nodded, cautiously.

'I'm told he hangs out down near the border with Mexico. Is that so?'

'I am told that also, *señor.*'

'You think you could find him if I send you down there, and do it pronto?'

'I will try, if you wish it.'

'I do. I'll give you money. Get a fresh horse from the remuda. I want you to travel fast and give a message to Buck. Don't come back without him, you understand?'

'What if he does not wish to come with me, *señor*?'

'For the kind of money I'm offering him, he will. Just get him back here, fast!'

That same afternoon Luna sped out of Teague's ranch on one of his fastest horses. He had a two-week ride ahead of him and meant to do it in one if he could. Senor Teague would look favorably upon his early return.

Jack Buck had already garnered a reputation as an unrepentant killer even before exiting his teen years. Buck's father Billy, was a traveling country preacher taking his wife Esmeralda and young Jack with him, roaming from town to town, preaching from the tailgate of their horse-drawn wagon home. Buck sold little silver chains and crosses guaranteed to connect their wearer to God's ear in times of strife, confusion and need of guidance. If stronger medicine was needed, he backed these up with small vials of Holy Water he absolutely guaranteed were

28

filled from springs in the Promised Land. If the supply ran low and had to be refilled crossing the nearest creek, that would do just as well. Why shake the faith of true believers and miss another four-dollar sale?

Billy Buck harangued those gathered to hear him, with fire and brimstone, threatening listeners about the wages of sin they were all sure to pay if they didn't change their errant ways. When it came to sin, Buck was a man speaking from vast experience. After leaving each town, out traveling, he had the habit of pulling a bottle of Old Tayler rye whiskey from back of the wagon, draining it.

'A demon . . . lives in this . . . bottle.' He once told young Jack, while weaving on the wagon seat, 'Don't you ever . . . let him touch your . . . lips, or I'll take a . . . whip to you!'

Buck took out his alcoholic rage and delusions on his wife, physically beating her and sometimes, even Jack too. One evening during one of his wild drinking sprees, Jack tried to intervene, begging his father to stop hitting his mother cowering on her knees with both hands over her face trying to ward off his blows. Billy turned, throwing a flurry of wild punches, knocking Jack to the carpeted wagon floor, before turning his brutal attention back to Esmeralda. A pistol was kept on a side shelf under some bedding. Jack lunged for it, got it. Turning, he yelled one more time for Billy to stop. When he didn't, Jack lifted the little gun at arm's length, pulling the trigger, sending a .36 caliber lead bullet into his father's skull, killing him instantly. Before the gun-smoke cleared away, Jack Buck learned the simple act of pulling a trigger was a fast, effective way to get results he wanted. If he could kill his own father so easily, strangers would mean nothing at all.

Jack practised constantly over the next two years until he became fast and accurate with a cross draw, right hand

29

reaching over his body to pull the pistol on his left side, kept in the holster, butt forward. He also started carrying a small hide-out derringer in his knee-high boots for backup. He began building a reputation for himself as someone available for hire, selling his gun-speed to powerful men with money who wanted competition either run out of the country or eliminated completely. Burl Teague would be his newest customer.

In nine days of hard riding, Alviso Luna found Buck in the border town of Juarez, immediately handing over Teague's message. Jack thumbed through the packet of cash as down-payment, reading the note while sitting in a smoke-filled cantina. Looking up at Luna, he had only one question.

'When do we leave?'

'*Mañana*,' the vaquero answered.

Up north at the Cox ranch, Arlee told all his cowboys to stay out of Mesquite after the killing shootout involving Link and Bull. But Link was quick to ask his boss how he intended to get supplies from town following those orders.

'Listen to me, you two,' Cox eyed Bonner and Bull. 'I know you did what you had to, but Teague won't let it end there. No matter how long it takes him, he'll try to get even with me. I can guarantee you that. All of us will have to be a lot more careful and alert of everything we do, both here and out working the longhorns. Going into town is just asking for trouble.'

Link shook his head, speaking up. 'You can't let Teague or Waite run us out of town. We've got as much right to be in there as anyone else. I made that clear to that tin-horn sheriff, when I was there. You let them do that to you now and it will only get worse because they'll know they can scare you off.'

Arlee didn't answer for a moment. He knew Link was right, yet a range war might hang in the balance, which could wipe him out financially, not to mention more senseless killing. He was in a tight spot and knew it. He pulled at his chin, trying to come up with an answer that would make sense to the men gathered around him.

'Listen, Link, I understand what you're saying, and I might even have to agree with some of it, but I can't afford to take any chances making it worse. You have to understand that. We didn't start this trouble but now we're all right in the big middle of it. Why go in to town and start it all over again? You might be fast with a six-gun, but the rest of these men are working cowboys, not gunfighters.'

'And what are you going to do when you need more supplies? Hide out?' Link countered. 'Good isn't going to haul them all the way out here. He can't leave the store because he's the only one in it. How about that? When you need more, just send me and Bull in? No one is going to mess with us, including Waite.'

'I'll think about it,' the boss man slowly shook his head in dismay. 'I just don't see any easy way out of all this.'

'There isn't. You either live your life and run this ranch the way you want, or get run over by someone like Teague. I can't see any reason to let that happen,' Link finished.

Once Luna and Buck started their fast ride north, neither spoke much during the day except at brief stops to rest and water the horses. One evening five days later around a small campfire, Buck pulled out Teague's note. Finished reading it, he eyed the Mexican's broad, brown face, over flickering flames.

'This boss man of yours must be a rich man to send you

all the way down here to fetch me. Aren't there any men up north with enough backbone to pull a trigger and solve this problem of his?'

'Maybe not, I don't know. Señor Teague does have many *vacas.*'

'He does, huh? Well he better have, because this little ride is going to cost him plenty. I'll see to that personally.'

Luna eyed the smiling gringo, but this time did not answer.

CHAPTER THREE

When Jack Buck first walked into Teague's office after arriving at the ranch, the powerful cattleman wasn't all that impressed with the man standing in front of him. Buck was only of average height, lanky to the point of being skinny. His clothes and long riding coat were dusty and wrinkled. But when he unbuttoned his coat, Teague saw the gun rig he wore with his six-gun butt forward on his left hip. He'd never seen another man carry like that before. If none of this enforced the feeling he'd hired the right man for the job, one other thing did. Buck's eyes. They seemed merely dark slits that bored right through whoever he was looking at and never seemed to blink. He didn't stick out his hand or so much as crack a smile, before sitting down opposite Teague's big oak desk, staring at the rancher.

'Your Mexican says you need me up here. Does your problem have a name? The sooner I know what's going on, the faster I can finish up our business here.'

Buck's voice was cold, without emotion, direct and straight to the point. Teague immediately liked his brevity. A man that didn't bandy words was someone who meant to move fast and decisively. It dispelled any doubt he'd hired the right man for the job.

'All right, I'll get to it.' Burl leaned back in his chair studying Buck intently. 'I've got unwanted competition in my business which is cattle. His name is Arlee Cox. His place is across the Big Muddy, about an hour's ride from here. One of his new cowboys, a man named Link Bonner, shot and killed my only son, Rory, over some trumped-up cattle charge. Then he went into town and shot down two of my men for no reason at all. He's a mad dog that has to be stopped and fast. It's just that simple. I want him killed. If Cox happens to get in the way, you can kill him too. I mean to own this range and every blade of grass on it. No one is going to stop me. Not even the death of my son.'

'If I take down Cox too, that will cost you another thousand dollars.'

'That's fine. Money is no object. Results are what I want.'

Buck didn't say anything for several moments, thinking over the name that Teague had mentioned. 'Bonner, huh? I've never heard that name before.' He shook his head. 'Things sometimes happen like this. Some peckerwood cowboy comes along and gets lucky. All of a sudden people think he's a hot gun-hand until someone faces him and ends that idea real quick. I'm that someone. You got a sheriff in that town I rode by, coming up here?'

'Yes, but he's my cousin. You don't have to worry about him getting in the way of your work. I'll see to that. You can stay out here at my ranch if you like. I've got plenty of room.'

'No, I want to stay in town, especially if this cowboy killer shows up. It will save me a lot of time having to hunt him down. You have a hotel?'

'Yes, it's not much, but it'll do. Tell Waite, my cousin, to take you there. I'll pay all the bills. Just tell them to charge it to me.'

As Teague predicted, the Longhorn Hotel had seen better days. The wooden, two-story structure was unpainted, its siding warped with age and weather. Austin Waite escorted Buck into the dingy foyer, up to an empty counter with a little bell atop it. He rang it while calling out.

'Hey Archie, get yourself out here. You got some business to take care of!'

The shuffle of slow feet was followed by an elderly, bald-headed man pushing curtains aside, coming out of a back room, eyeing the two men.

'You don't have to yell at me, Waite. I ain't deaf yet ya' know.'

'Well if you ain't, you soon will be. This man is Jack Buck. He's a guest of my cousin Burl Teague. You charge his bill to Burl. He's paying for everything, you understand?'

'With his money, I ain't surprised,' the old man countered.

'I didn't ask you for any smart mouth. Just see to it the bills go to him.'

Archie Stipe shrugged without answering for a moment before he thought of something else. 'You want a fresh towel every day, that's a dollar extra.'

'Just shut up and give him whatever he wants!' Waite browbeat the old man.

'I want a room on the second floor facing the street,' Buck finally spoke up.

Stipe turned back to the keyboard, studying it up close without his glasses. 'Let's see . . . I believe . . . number five might work, or maybe . . . number seven?'

Waite pushed around the counter, elbowing Stipe out

of the way. 'Here, number five is open.' He handed the key to Buck.

'You have to sign in, too.' Stipe wasn't done, pointing at the yellowed pages of the register.

'He isn't signing anything. He's Burl's guest, like I told you. Can't you get that through your thick head?'

'But that's the rules,' Stipe protested.

'We don't care about any rules. Now shut up and go back to sleep.' Waite turned the old man around, shoving him back through the curtains as he mumbled something under his breath.

'You need anything else, come down to my office,' Waite told Buck. 'I gotta get back to work. I can stay in town tonight if you want and take you out to eat. We've got two good places for a decent meal.'

'No, I want to look around for myself. But I would like to know if this Bonner comes into town on a regular basis?'

'No, not regular. I guess when they need supplies out at Cox's place he shows up, but that's about it. There's no telling when that might be.'

'Then you need to give him a good reason to do so. Deliver a message, you want to make peace or anything else you can think of. I don't want to sit around here wasting time. He might not show up for weeks. If he goes for it, you point him out to me then get out of the way. I'll take care of the rest of it.'

'All right. I'll send someone out there and let you know if they answer or not.'

'Do it today. My time is money. I want to take care of him and get out of this miserable town. I've already seen enough to know I don't want to stay any longer than I have to. There's also wanted paper out on me this far north. I don't want anyone else to get brave and try to collect on that either.'

The sun was only a dim, opaque disk behind grey clouds when young Eddy Hopkins, a part-time worker at the Red Racer livery stable in town, rode up to the Cox ranch-house at full gallop.

Arlee heard the horse coming in. Getting up from his desk he went outside on the front porch as the teenager pulled to a stop.

'Eddy, what are you doing way out here?' Cox asked.

Hopkins stepped down out of the saddle, climbing the porch steps, handing Arlee the note. 'Sheriff Waite told me to get this to you fast. He even gave me five dollars to deliver it.'

'Five dollars? It must be pretty important for him to spend that kind of money.'

'Must be. He told me to wait for your answer, too.'

Arlee unfolded the paper, reading the note to himself. Finishing, he looked up at the kid. 'I'm going to write my answer on the other side, so you don't have to try and remember what I said. You give it to Waite soon as you get back to town, OK?'

'Yes, sir, I sure will, Mr Cox.'

After Eddy left, Arlee immediately saddled up a horse, riding out to his herd of longhorns, searching for Link. Approaching one of his men he called out, 'You seen Bonner?'

'I think he's over on the north end.' The cowboy pointed.

'All right, thanks.' He kicked his horse away.

Link saw his boss riding in, waving a hand over his head. Tate, close by, also pointed him out. When he reached the pair of men, Link was first to speak.

'You made a long ride out here. Must be something important.'

'It is.' Cox nodded, a serious look coming over his face. 'Waite wants you and me to come into town and meet with him tomorrow morning. He says he wants to talk peace between us and Teague. I don't know what to make of it. It doesn't sound like anything Teague would do, but I think we ought to at least go find out.'

Link stared back without answering right away. When he did, it was with open suspicion. 'I don't know Teague like you do, but I know this. He's already tried to kill you once and maybe he wants another chance using his lawman as an alibi.'

'I never wanted any of this to go this far. This might be my only chance to end it. That's not something easy to walk away from, Link.'

'If you two are going in, I want to ride with you,' Bull spoke up. 'Teague might have a dozen men in there just waiting to ambush both of you, and that two-bit sheriff is one of them.'

'I don't know, Bull.' Cox shook his head. 'I don't want three of us riding into town like we've come looking for a fight. Waite only asked for me and Link. I think we ought to keep it that way, even if we do have to take a chance at it.'

'A chance? You can't trust those birds any farther than I could throw them with one hand. I say don't do it, either one of you. Someone is going to catch a bullet.'

The three men stood looking at each other without speaking until Arlee finally had the last word. 'I've got to try and settle this once and for all. Link and I will go in like I said. We'll be careful, don't worry none about that.'

Eddy Hopkins rode back into Mesquite, pulling to a

halt in front of Sheriff Waite's office. Getting down, he rushed up to the door, stepping inside to find Waite sitting at his desk emptying out a box of .45 caliber cartridges.

'I delivered your note like you said, Sheriff.' Eddy stood at his desk.

'Did you get an answer?'

'Yes, sir, I did. Here it is.' He handed the note over as Waite leaned forward taking the crumpled paper, reading it silently to himself.

'You did real good, kid. Now get back to the Red Racer, and do your job. That's all I needed from you.'

Eddy headed for the door with a smile on his face and a shiny, five-dollar gold piece in his pocket. He couldn't wait to get home after work and show his mother the money he'd made. Waite was only seconds behind him, out the door heading for the Longhorn Hotel.

Jack Buck was standing at the window in his room, watching people move on the street below, when a knock on the door turned him away. He crossed the room, pulling his six-gun from the holster hung on a brass bed post. At the door he put one hand on the handle, cocking the pistol with the other. 'Who is it?' he called out.

'It's me, Waite. Let me in.'

Once inside, the sheriff handed Buck the note. 'Looks like he went for it,' he said.

A slow smile came over Buck's face, before handing it back.

'That was almost too easy. I'll be out of town, on my way back south before noon the way this is going. Your cousin better be ready to pay me double with Bonner and his boss coming in. I'll drop both of them at the same time.'

'I'm going to ride out to Burl's ranch and tell him what's about to happen. He might want to be here to see it for himself.'

'You do that. And tell him I won't even charge him extra for the show.'

The first meager slash of dawn painted the eastern sky in a thin, grey line as Link sat at a table in the bunkhouse, cleaning his .45. Bull sat opposite him, sipping a cup of hot, black coffee, off the crackling pot-bellied stove.

'You still mean to go through with this?' Bull couldn't stay quiet any longer. 'None of it makes any sense to me. You know that, don't you?'

'I can't let Arlee go in there alone, can I?'

'Well, maybe not, but why not take some help in with you? You know I'll go, and so will some other men, if you'll just ask them.'

'No, they won't. They're not gun-hands and they know it. They're not getting paid to stand up against anyone who might want to put a bullet in them. I don't blame them either.'

'What if Teague has half a dozen men waiting for you and Cox to come in? You think you can come out on top in a dog-fight like that? I sure don't.'

'I don't think Teague is dumb enough to take a chance like that. He may own his sheriff, but there's more law in other places, like US Marshals and even the Army that could come after him. There's something else in the wind. I just don't know what yet. I know it isn't Waite alone. He's nothing but an empty star. He isn't going to pull on anyone. We both saw that already.'

'What else then?'

'I don't know, but I imagine I'll find out pretty quick.' He finished slowly reloading all six cylinders with grey-domed bullets, when the door suddenly opened and Arlee

Cox walked in.

'Morning boys. You about ready to ride, Link?'

'I am.' Bonner got to his feet, noticing Cox had a pistol strapped on his hip. 'Can I suggest something to you, Arlee?'

'Sure, what it is?'

'Leave your pistol here.'

'What for?'

'You said it yourself. You don't want us to look like we're coming in spoiling for a fight, do you?'

'You've got yours on.'

'I always do. You don't. Leave it this time. I've got enough gun for both if we need it. This is supposed to be a peace meeting, remember?'

Cox looked from Bonner to Bull, slowly unbuckling the gun-belt, laying the rig on a bunk bed. 'If you think it's best, I'll do it.' He nodded.

'I do. Let's get saddled up and ride in.' Link headed for the door.

Burl Teague stood by the window in the sheriff's office, looking out on a nearly empty street, before turning back to his cousin and Jack Buck. 'The note said they'd be here at eight o'clock. It's eight now and no one has showed. Have they turned yellow already?'

'They'll be here,' Waite promised. 'It might take them a little longer, but they'll come in. Cox made that clear in his answer. He wants to settle this, real bad. We'll just have to wait them out.'

Buck sat propped on the edge of the desk with his legs crossed, unconcerned about the clock on the wall. He'd gotten up early, packed his saddle bags, and was ready to begin the ride south once he finished his job. Glancing at the cattle man, he reminded him about the extra thousand dollars if he took down Cox, too.

'I'll kill this Bonner first and his boss second. You better have that extra money on you, Teague.'

'Don't you worry about the cash. I've got it. First I want to see you in action.'

'Don't blink or you might miss the whole show. I mean to be long gone from this town before noon.'

Twenty minutes dragged by, then thirty. Waite paced the floor, going to the window, looking out then turning back to check the clock again, before going to his desk, dropping in the chair with a grunt, staring at both men. Three minutes later he was up again nervously following the same routine.

'You better sit down,' Buck ridiculed. 'You're wearing a hole in the floor.'

Waite looked at Buck but didn't answer before sitting down again. Small beads of perspiration began popping out on his broad, whiskered face. The thought of being in the middle of another gunfight had his stomach boiling in knots. He'd seen Bonner in action. He knew how fast he was, even if Buck scoffed at the notion some Texas Tornado could outdraw him.

'I . . . just hope you don't expect me to be out there when Buck and Bonner go at it.' He turned to Teague, praying he'd agree.

'Yes, I do. That's what I'm paying you for. You're what's going to make this deal look real. When Cox sees you, he'll think everything is all right.'

'But I'm no gunfighter, Burl. You know that. That ain't my job and never has been. That's Buck's business.'

'You'll do what I tell you to. I don't want this messed up at the last minute because you've suddenly lost your guts. After they face off, you can run for it. Not until, you understand!'

'Wait a minute, Burl. We're blood kin. I'm your. . . .'

'There's no buts about it. Stop your damn whining or I'll send you back where I found you, dipping sheep for a living!'

Teague turned back to the clock, red-faced from the tongue-lashing he'd given his cousin. 'It's already nine. Where are they? I won't be surprised if no one shows up at all. This has just been a waste of my time!'

Buck pushed off the desk as Teague left the window to cross the room then sit in the chair opposite the desk. Leaning on the window frame, Buck looked out onto the street. Waite had put the word out, there was going to be big trouble. Most store-fronts remained shuttered, their owners at home waiting for things to calm down tomorrow. The boardwalks were nearly empty except for the occasional figure of a lone man quick stepping across the street from one saloon to another. Another ten minutes passed before Buck broke the silence with a question.

'What kind of horse does this Cox ride?'

'I think he has a dappled mare, one of them odd looking animals from Mexico,' Waite answered.

'What about Bonner?'

'I'm not sure. Maybe a big, dark horse with a sort of white star on its forehead. I wasn't paying much attention to what he was riding last time he came in here. Why are you asking?'

'Because they're riding down the street, coming into town right now.'

Teague and Waite scrambled to the window, crowding in to look out. 'That's them, sure enough.' Waite's voice was strained with tension. 'I told you they'd show up, didn't I, I told ya!'

'Come on.' Buck grabbed Waite by his arm, heading for the front door. 'I want to stop them in the middle of the street out in the open.'

'There's Waite, but I don't see Teague.' Cox nodded, both riders coming closer as two men stepped out of the sheriff's office into the street.

'That's far enough. Stop right there!' Buck called out holding up one hand. 'Get off those horses. I've got a message for you from Burl Teague.'

'Who is that with Waite?' Cox asked. 'I've never seen him before.'

'From the look of him and that gun rig he's got strapped on, I'd say Teague hired himself a fast-gun. The only way anything is going to be settled now is with six-guns. When we get down, you take the horses and get out of the way fast. I'll end this between him and me.'

'No, don't do it, Link. This isn't what I came into town for. I don't want any more killing. Let's turn around and head back to the ranch. It's not worth this.'

'Too late for that now. You can't walk away from this one. Just get out of the way like I said. Do it, Arlee.'

Waite saw Cox hesitate before Link handed him the reins to his horse, pushing him away. 'I've done my part.' His voice was a tense whisper to Buck. 'And that's all I'm going to do.' He began backing toward the boardwalk, lifting both hands shoulder high to show he wasn't any part of any showdown.

Buck took a few careful steps forward, closing the distance as he sized up this man he'd heard so much about. He decided to have a little fun before he killed him.

'You know who I am, Bonner?' he called out.

Link didn't answer. Instead he moved even closer until

both men stood thirty feet away, facing each other.

'No, but I know your kind. You're either a back-shooter, or someone who likes to make a name for himself killing drunken cowboys. The bone-yard is full of misfits like you. Pretty quick they'll dig a hole for you too.'

Buck bristled at the stinging insult. 'I'm Jack Buck, you fool. At least you ought to know who shot you down while you're bleeding out on the ground!'

'Teague better have paid you enough for a coffin. That's the last dollar anyone is going to waste on a savage like you.'

Buck's face fell to a stony stare. Bonner wasn't going to run or back down. All that was left was to kill him.

Jack Buck was fast, real fast. Those that saw him in action said his gun-hand moved so quick it was just a blur. It was just as fast that morning out on the street in Mesquite, facing Link Bonner. But this time it wasn't quite fast enough. His six-gun had just cleared the holster when Link's .45 thundered in two spears of flame, the bullets hitting Buck in the stomach and chest, driving the hired killer backwards as he sank to his knees. His face twisted in pain and disbelief. The pistol slipped from his hands. Link steadied his six-gun for a third shot. It wasn't needed. Jack Buck, the second-fastest gun in the Indian Nation, collapsed in a heap, dead in the street.

Those two thundering pistol shots sealed the fate of Link Bonner too, and in a way he could have never imagined. His name would begin to circulate through every cow town, mining camp and tent city across the west. His life had suddenly changed, whether he liked it or not. It was the fate of any man who had earned the name of the fastest six-gun around, and the will to use it. Bonner's days working cattle, traveling freely wherever he wanted, just another cowboy riding into town, were over. Men of wealth and position would suddenly know his name. They could use a man like Link Bonner to achieve their own ends. Money was no object. The west was wide open for those bold enough, cunning enough and powerful enough to seize it, building empires of their own. Link Bonner was a man who could make that happen, if he decided to.

Bull Tate sat back in his chair at the High Timber Saloon in Mountain Gate, to the rapt attention of the crowd of men gathered around him, listening to every word of his story. Reaching over, he poured another shot of Old Taylor, savoring it a moment before downing it.

'And that's where it all started for my friend Link Bonner.' He eyed the young cowboys. 'From there everything else just took off like a whirlwind.'

'What happened to Burl Teague?' one listener wondered.

'Teague was done trying to run Cox out of business or hiring anyone else to try after Buck. He stayed on his side of the Big Muddy after that. He was killed about three years later when one of his prized bulls got out and he tried to run it back in. The old longhorn charged his horse, knocking it down on top of him. Broke his neck. He had no close kin. His son was already dead. Some distant uncle back east came out and sold off the ranch and all the cattle, then took the stage back home. I guess he didn't much like the smell of range cattle. He made it clear he had to get back to civilization, clean sheets and frilly women. For Link, the die was cast. He had a gunfighter's name he never could shed even if he wanted to. Sometimes it worked out for the best, and sometimes not so good. Eventually, he realized he'd spend the rest of his life making a living using his six-gun. I'm glad I had the chance to ride with him some of those wide, open days. I never met another man comes close to him. I sure don't expect to today the way the west has changed. I'll say this, though. Time sure didn't pass Link Bonner by. He rode it like a wild mustang and made the most of it while he was here.'

'What happened after Teague died? Did you and Link stay down there at the Cox ranch?' another man in the gathering asked.

'No, we picked up our pay checks and rode out. Arlee wanted us to stay real bad, but Link said we were done. It was best if we moved on. Maybe he thought he could outride the reputation that was bound to be coming. He never said so out loud, but I always thought that was the reason. We headed north, far from Indian Territory where he figured no one would know him. But news like the showdown in Mesquite travels faster than a West Texas wind. We weren't going to leave anything behind. It came right along with us.'

CHAPTER FOUR

Link and Bull were almost three weeks out of town somewhere in what would become Colorado Territory, when
they ran into five riders pretty much by accident. One look
up close was enough to know all five were nothing but
trouble. They looked like they were on the run from something, all dusty and dirty, clothes worn thin. Even their
horses looked worn out. Likely from being run long and
hard. The pair never saw them until it was too late. Out
there you never saw anyone but an occasional Indian
hunting party. It was really a no man's land. No towns, no
roads, mostly game trails to travel on. Bull and Link rode
up out of a dry wash right into them. The group must have
seen the two a long way out and hid until they showed.
The first thing they saw were pistols and a shotgun leveled
on them.

'Dump them six-guns, and I mean real fast!' one man
barked, who looked like the leader.

Bull wondered if Link was going to try to pull on the
outlaws, facing all that hardware, but the odds were too
big against them. Even if they did take down one or two,
they'd still come out on the short end.

'Who are you two and what are you doing out here?
Talk fast and you better make it good.'

48

'We're just passing through,' Bull answered. 'We're not looking for any trouble.'

'What's your name?'

'Does that matter out here?' Link said.

'Yeah, it might if you're lawmen or bounty-hunters.'

'We're neither one. Just riding north,' Bull came back.

'You sure you didn't ride out of Arroyo Grande with reward money on your mind?'

'We've never been to Arroyo Grande, and don't know about any reward.'

One of the men picked up Link's and Bull's pistols, handing them to Dirk Shin, doing all the talking. Shin hefted the heavy iron in both hands, still studying the two men thoughtfully. 'I still want a name,' he insisted.

Bull glanced at Link who nodded slightly. 'Mine's Tate. My partner here is Bonner.'

Shin looked around at his men, waiting for someone to speak up. 'Any of you ever heard of these two?' All he got back were blank stares, prompting Bull to continue trying to talk their way out of it.

'We just finished up herding longhorns down south and rode up this way. We don't know about any towns or anything else up here. We haven't even seen a town in three weeks.'

'Just a couple of long-lost cow punchers, huh?' Shin still eyed the pair suspiciously. 'Maybe, maybe not. Dory, get those saddle bags off their horses and dump everything out on the ground. You two sit real still while I take a look.'

The skinny, whiskered man untied both leather bags, unbuckling then turning them upside down, spilling the contents. Kneeling, he picked through ponchos, extra clothes and loose cartridges. Two leather pouches held Link and Bull's last pay from Cox.

'Nothin' worth anything except this money.' He straightened up, handing Shin both pouches, who poured some of the coins out into one hand, before twisting in the saddle and emptying both into his saddle bags.

'You two are going to need another job, real quick now you're flat broke!' Dirk smiled with a low laugh. He emptied the bullets out of both six-guns before tossing them on the ground. 'You better get on your way, and I don't want to see either one of you again. I could have left you laying out here in the sagebrush for vultures. Call it your lucky day. We've got other things on our mind. Now get going!'

Link and Bull picked up their six-guns, starting away while Shin and his men watched them go until out of sight.

'Something ain't right about those two,' one of Shin's men spoke up, leaning on the saddle horn. 'I can't put my finger on it. That one called Bonner never said much. He let the big man do all the talking. I don't like a quiet man. You never know what he's thinking.'

'I wouldn't worry much about it now. What we've got to do is keep our necks out of a hanging rope, after that bank job in Arroyo Grande. If you and Dory hadn't shot up the place and killed that bank teller, we'd be a lot better off without a murder charge hanging over us. When are you going to get it through that thick head of yours to follow orders when I give them instead of going off mad dog.'

'He was going for a counter gun. What was I suppose to do, stand there and get shot down?'

Shin didn't answer this time. Running into Bonner and Bull when he thought he and his men were in the clear, way out here, had him wondering if he should change plans. He took one more long look in the direction the two men had just left and made up his mind. 'We're going west instead of north. I changed my mind.'

Link and Tate only rode far enough away to be out of sight of the gang before Link pulled to a stop. Reaching into his saddle bags he reloaded his six-gun, telling Bull to do the same. Once finished, he stood in the stirrups, looking back.

'Why are we stopping?' Bull questioned.

'Soon as they're far enough away, we're turning around, following them.'

'What for? We were lucky to get off like we did.'

'I want my money back. It's all we've got. I'm not going to give it up because they got the drop on us. That won't happen twice.'

'You want to take on all five of them?'

'Yes, when the time is right.'

'When would that be?'

'Tonight, after dark when they stop to make camp.'

Bull sat in the saddle, dumbfounded by his pal's bravado. Link actually thought the two of them could take on all five men and finish on top, come hell or high water. Before he could try to talk some sense into Link, his friend had more to say about his plan.

'We'll stay back far enough to see which way they're going. When they make camp, we'll give them another hour to fall asleep. Then we'll make our move.'

Bull started to argue the point then gave up, shaking his head while looking at his partner in awe.

The late afternoon sun was burning its way down into flat-topped mesas, when Sheriff K.C. Hollis and his posse of eight men rode back into Arroyo Grande, dusty, tired and dejected. They'd trailed the bank robbers all that day until running out of tracks on flinty ground. The gang had fled at a breakneck pace, pushing their horses on a run the posse could not match. Hollis pulled to a stop in front of his office where a knot of men quickly formed around him, eager for information on what had happened. Even before easing out of the saddle, they were barking questions.

'Did you catch up to them, Sheriff?' one man shouted.

Hollis slowly shook his head as people pushed closer.

'Was there a gun fight?' another wondered out loud.

'We never actually got them in sight. We had to trail them on tracks. Once they ran out, we pretty much lost them. They had too much of a head start on us. Looks like they were headed north. Now there's no telling where they went. They must have jackrabbit blood in them the way they scattered so fast. Was anyone else hurt in the bank holdup? I didn't have time to ask when we rode out.'

'You know the bank teller, Terry Roberts was killed, but Mrs Thatcher caught a bullet in the leg. Otto Jenson was also wounded. They're both down at the doctor's office. Looks like they'll pull through, though,' someone volunteered.

'Why can't you get a US Marshal out here to go after those murderers if you can't catch up to them?' A woman in the back of the crowd spoke up. 'We all had our money in the bank and now it's gone. It isn't safe for decent folks to walk the streets these days with things like this going on!'

'There isn't a marshal within forty miles of here, Mrs Leslie. You and your husband can walk the streets without worrying about being molested. This gang isn't from around here. They must be a bunch of jay-hawks moving through,' Hollis answered.

'Listen, Hollis, we voted to put you in office on the

notion you'd keep the town safe from murderers like this. And that includes protecting our hard-earned money, too. You've got to do something more about it than just say they got away!' another shouted.

'Listen to me before you get yourself all riled up further. This bunch will end up caught someplace else. They always do. When they do, I can try to get some of your money back. All I have is a volunteer posse who want to get home each night to a hot dinner, warm fireplace and their wives and kids. I can't go after these men for days or weeks trying to run them down. Right now I'm tired and need some rest too. Soon as I get my horse down to the livery stable, I'm going home myself.'

'Wait a minute, Sheriff. Why don't you put up some reward money to help catch this bunch?' a tall man wearing a bowler hat shouted.

'Yeah,' another seconded. 'Money sure might work. Especially if there's enough of it. Maybe the businesses here in town would pitch in some cash?'

'And if there's enough of it, there might even be more reward money from other towns or even banks if they've been robbed too?' a bystander suggested.

'All right, all right.' Hollis held up his hand, trying to calm everyone down. 'I'll talk to some of the store owners tomorrow and see if they're willing to do that. Right now, why doesn't everyone go home. We've had enough suggestions for one day.'

Bonner and Tate rode well back out of sight of Shin and his men the remainder of that day, until the long shadows of evening overtook them, with no chance to move closer. The gang made camp on an elevated plateau where they could look over their back trail. The two men were forced to try sleeping, rolled up in their saddle-blankets without a fire that might give them away. At dawn they lay shivering against the bitter cold.

'I'd give a whole lot to have a good fire going right now. I'm about half froze to death.' Bull sat up, pulling the heavy blanket over his shoulders and hat down lower on his head.

'You know we can't do that. Shin's less than a half-mile away. They'd spot smoke fast. They don't know they're being followed. That's our ace in the hole. We can't lose it. We'll let them move out and give them enough time to put some distance between us again before we move. Maybe tonight we'll have a chance to take them in a better spot. One thing is for sure.'

'What's that?'

'At least out here they aren't spending any of our money. There's no town to spend it in. Let's saddle the horses. We can also move around a bit and try to warm up.'

All that day the two trackers followed the gang, staying out of sight, keeping to canyon bottoms and brushy dry washes. Every hour or so, Link would pull to a stop and dismount, climbing high enough on foot to peek ahead, seeing the distant images of riders moving steadily away. At sundown the five made camp in a copse of scraggy cottonwoods, building a good-size fire to ward off the night cold, certain they'd left any chance of trouble far behind. Link and Tate tied their horses off well out from their camp. Waiting until dark, they moved closer on foot quietly until they could hear the pop and crackle of fire through the tall brush ahead before they could actually see the men. At a crouch they covered the last few yards, six-guns clutched in their hands. Shin was standing next to leaping flames with a coffee cup in his hand, the other four men sitting with their backs to them, eating. Bull glanced at Link. The glow from the firelight was enough to see him nod before straightening up with a shout.

'Get up and keep your hands up where I can see them!'

The sudden reaction was instant and chaotic. Shin dropped the coffee cup, pulling for his pistol. Link fired twice, sending him spinning to the ground with a howl of pain. The other men dove for cover behind saddles, frantically trying to draw pistols as both men ran forward shooting fast at close range, the gun flashes lighting up the night sky. Two of the gang rolled on the ground, twisting with bullet hits while the remaining pair, still on their knees, threw up their hands, shouting out loud not to kill them.

Link quickly stepped around the roaring fire, standing over Dirk Shin lying on his back, face contorted in pain, holding his arm with one hand while blood oozed out between his fingers.

'I . . . should'a killed you when . . . I had the chance,' Shin hissed through clenched teeth.

'We all make mistakes. Yours was stealing my money. I've come to get it back. Get on your feet!' He reached down, pulling Shin up face to face, both men glaring at each other.

'Bull, you got the other two?' Bonner shouted.

'Yeah, I got 'em. Their pals are done for and these two don't want to join them.'

Link herded the remaining three men next to the fire with an order to Bull. 'Tie them up, including Shin. We're taking them back to Arroyo Grande. I got the feeling folks there might be eager to get their hands on them. We'll take turns sitting up over them tonight. I'll take first watch.'

'What about me . . . I might bleed to death like this!' Shin screamed, his eyes red with hate.

'Then we'll only have two to bring in,' Bonner answered. 'Bull, tie something over his arm to stop the bleeding. That's all he's getting, while I empty their saddle bags and get our money back.'

'What about the two dead ones?'

'We'll rope them over their horses and bring them with us. Someone might know who they are or there could be paper on the whole bunch. We'll find that out when we reach Arroyo Grande.'

Five days later, people on the street were stopped dead in their tracks, pointing and gesturing at the eerie procession that rode into town, sending one excited man running for the sheriff's office, shouting Hollis' name at the top of his lungs.

Bonner rode in the lead, Shin and his two men still alive, tied with their hands behind their backs, following him. Tate came fifth, pulling two more horses with the bodies of the last gang members roped face-down over their saddles. A throng of people immediately began following the riders down main street, shouting questions at Bonner.

'Who are you, mister? A federal marshal?' one called out, pacing the horsemen.

Link shook his head and kept riding without answering.

'Isn't that the Shin gang?' another suggested. 'We didn't get much of a look at them when they rode out of town shooting up the place, but that does look a lot like what I remember.'

'That's what's left of them.' Link pulled a thumb over his shoulder while Dirk sat stone-faced, staring straight ahead.

'Did you get our money back? They took almost every dime in the bank. We've got nothing left!' a new voice joined the chorus.

Link reached around with one hand slapping the bulging saddle bags. A cheer of joy erupted from the crowd the same moment Sheriff Hollis stepped out on the front porch of his office, wondering what all the commotion was about. Looking down the street he saw the long line of riders approaching and the throng of people gathered around them. Squinting against the sun, he tried to make out the man in the lead as Link rode closer, pulling to a stop in front of him but staying in the saddle.

'You must be the sheriff,' he eyed the star on Hollis' vest. 'I've got Dirk Shin and what's left of his men here. The two saddle-bags behind me are full of money I assume was stolen from your bank. I took out fifty dollars Shin stole from me and my partner behind me there with those two bodies.'

Hollis stood awe struck, at a loss for words. He couldn't believe the stroke of luck that brought the gang back to town, even if he couldn't run them down. It was even harder to believe that just these two men alone had taken all five of the gang without getting shot to pieces. It took another moment before he could speak up.

'Who are you two and what's your name? Are you some kind of lawmen or bounty-hunters?'

'No.' Link shook his head as the crowd pressed closer, not to miss a single word. 'Like I said, they stole the only money we had on us. I wasn't going to let them ride away and leave us flat broke. We tracked them until they thought they were in the clear, then took them after sundown.'

'When is someone going to get me a doctor!' Shin suddenly called out, turning all heads toward him. 'I'm bleeding to death here while you back-shooters talk your fool heads off!'

Hollis ordered one man in the crowd to go get Doctor Simms and another to get to the office of Myron Biddle, the undertaker. 'Tell Biddle to bring his buggy. He's got two bodies to take to his place.' He turned back to Bonner. 'You and your pal get down and come into my office. You've still got a lot of explaining to do about how all this happened.'

Hollis took Shin and his two men inside the office, locking them in separate cells while Dirk still screamed for a doctor. Closing the door to the cell-block to shut off the noise, the sheriff came back into the office, sitting opposite Link and Tate, carefully sizing up both men. Link briefly told him again how they were robbed of their last paycheck after leaving Arlee Cox's ranch down south. He made a point not to mention the shootout with Jack Buck on the street in Mesquite, for good reason. That would only bring more questions and suspicion about them. Hollis sat, legs crossed, listening intently to every word. The more Link talked, the more he couldn't believe how two out-of-work cowboys had the brass and backbone to take on an entire gang of five men just to get their last pay back.

When Link finished, the sheriff stood, unbuckling the saddle bags then pouring the stolen money out on the desk. He ran his hands through the cold silver and gold coins along with a lesser amount of paper money, as an idea began forming in his head. He knew people in town would not only be immensely grateful for the return of their hard-earned savings, but might also question why he and his posse could not run down the Shin gang, when just these two strangers did. They might also decide they had voted in the wrong man for sheriff and think they'd found his two new replacements. Hollis quickly came up with an idea of how to kill two birds with just one stone. He scooped the money back in the saddle bags. Sitting down looking from Bonner to Bull he made a surprising offer.

'Look you two. I have to hand it to you. You pulled off one hell of a job doing what you did. People around here are going to be real happy about it, when you could have taken the money and just kept riding. I've been needing a couple of deputies for quite a while. Obviously, you two could handle a job like that. Arroyo Grande is a pretty quiet town most of the time. What do you say to it? I can deputize both of you right now.'

Bull glanced at Link with an expression of surprise at the sudden offer. Bonner replied immediately.

'I don't think that's a job either of us would want. We're not lawmen and never have been.'

'Don't be too quick to say no. I can sweeten the pot by telling you that business men here in town put up a five-hundred dollar reward for the capture of Shin and his gang. Both of you were already five-hundred dollars richer before you rode into town. You can't make that kind of money prodding longhorns, can you?'

'Who pays us that?' Link ignored the statement.

'I do. I've got the money right here in my safe. And remember something else too. There could be more reward money coming from other towns or maybe even the territorial government. Shin and his bunch were on the run for a long time before you brought them down. They raised a lot of hell and shot up towns before we ever saw them here in Arroyo Grande.'

'We'll take the money, but we're still not interested in pinning on a badge. Bull and I go where we want when we want. A lawman has to stick in one place. It's likely we won't be here in town much longer than a few days. You'll have to find someone else for the job. It's not for us.'

Hollis cleared his throat, pushing back from the chair, crossing the room, kneeling at a small safe. He edged up close enough so the combination dial couldn't be seen by the others while spinning the numbers in. Back at the desk he laid the cash, mostly in paper money, with some coins on top. 'Here's your money. I still think you should reconsider. I'd be willing to pay each of you thirty-five dollars a month. That's more than most deputies make anyplace else plus this reward money. You could live pretty high like that.'

'You have a hotel here?' Bonner ignored the suggestion again.

'We do. It's the Mesa House down at the end of the street. They even have hot water tubs out back for an extra dollar a day.'

'Maybe we'll wash off some of this trail dust and get a few restaurant meals before we pull out. What about Shin and his men. Will they stand trial here?'

'Not likely. They'll end up in territorial prison down in Langley. They've got a federal judge and court house there to handle men like him. Half the men who go in there never come out alive between the disease, rats and killings inside. Either way he'll never see the light of day again once they put him behind bars. He's got you and your partner to thank for that.'

Shadows of evening covered Arroyo Grande, as Link sat back in the big wooden tub steaming with thermal water. He rested his head on a double-wrapped towel folded over the edge of the vessel. The back door to the Mesa House stood yards away. Bull sat in his tub, still wearing his wide-brimmed hat and red, long-John underwear, refusing to bathe naked.

'Why don't you try to relax and enjoy this?' Bonner suggested. 'Once we get back in the saddle, you'll wish you were here soaking up some of this heat.'

'I don't much care for this like you do. I feel more like a toad in a cook pot. It must be some kind of Indian water torture. And I don't like that old woman keeps coming in here trying to pour more hot water on me. I told her to stop it. I don't need any more.'

'That's her job. She can't see anything the way you're still dressed, and she wouldn't care if she could.'

'Well, it makes me feel uncomfortable having her around. Besides, I'd like to get out of here and go find myself a drink. I saw a saloon right across the street when we checked in. Let's dry off and go over there. If we ain't washed away all our sins by now, we never will!'

CHAPTER FIVE

Inside the Pueblo Cantina, a bald-headed man with a half lit cigar in his mouth sat at a piano against one wall, banging out the tune to 'Oh Susanna'. Link and Tate heard the rinky-tink music even before they pushed through the front door.

'Now this is more like it,' Bull exclaimed as they worked their way up to the bar through the noisy, smoke-filled room.

'What's your poison, gents?' The bar-keep, a big man wearing a dirty apron, came up eyeing his new customers before a sudden spark of recognition lit his whiskered face. 'Say, aren't you two the men who rode into town earlier pulling Shin and his boys all tied up like rodeo steers?'

Men up and down the bar heard the remark, craning their necks to get a better look. 'Yeah, that's them all right. I seen'm when they rode in, too!' one seconded, moving closer down the counter. More customers followed.

'Your drinks are on me,' the bar-man said. 'Put your money away. I had six-hundred dollars in that bank when Shin busted it wide open. You two saved my bacon doing what you did.' He pushed two stubby glasses across the counter, reaching under the bar for a bottle of whiskey with an unbroken seal.

'Sheriff Hollis couldn't catch up to that bunch even with half a dozen men!' another man spoke up. 'And you two did it by yourself. You must be a couple of rough boys, that's for sure. Kinda makes me wonder what good Hollis is, don't it?' Laughter exploded up and down the bar as a crowd of men surrounded the pair, hoping to hear how Shin was taken. But the sudden notoriety made Link strangely uncomfortable. He didn't like people he didn't know, getting that close to him personally. He let Tate do most of the talking. Before the evening ended, the two men had become the talk of the crowd at the Pueblo Cantina, along with the rest of Arroyo Grande. In following days, everywhere the two men went someone wanted to stop them to hear the story over and over. Link had enough. He announced to Bull they were leaving town the next morning after paying off the bill at Mesa House and making one final stop at Sheriff Hollis' office.

It was still early when the two men entered the sheriff's office. Hollis, in the cell corridor behind the main office, was with Doctor Simms putting a fresh dressing on Dirk Shin's swollen arm. Hollis heard the front door close when they came in. Leading the doctor outside the cell and locking it, he told Simms to finish the bandages through the bars while he headed for the office.

'Bonner, I heard you two are leaving town. Is that true?' he asked, stepping into the room with Doctor Simms moments behind him.

'We are. I came to let you know in case any more reward money shows up, I'll write you where to send it. Right now I don't know where or when that will be.'

'You sure you don't want that deputy's job I offered you two?'

'We're sure. It's not for us. When does Shin get moved?'

'Likely some time this week. They'll ride up from Langley to get him. I'll be glad to see him go. He's been nothing but trouble since you and your partner brought the whole bunch into town. I'm tired of his yelling and complaining all the time. If he knew you were out here he'd start it up all over again.'

As the sheriff talked, the good doctor got his first close-up look at Bonner and his sidekick. He'd only briefly seen the men out on the street, when first summoned after the pair brought the gang in. Like all good doctors do because of their trade, he studied Link Bonner more closely, sizing him up both physically and mentally from his conversation with Hollis. Slightly under six feet tall, tending to be thin rather than muscular, he seemed at first like most other men. But his mannerisms, the way he talked, those dark eyes that seemed to take in everything with one quick glance, spoke of a man who was cock-sure of himself and didn't care much about the opinions of others. Simms could see how and why Bonner went after Shin and his men just to get his pay back when most men would never chance it.

His *amigo*, Bull Tate, was the complete opposite of Bonner. Physically a much larger man to the point of being nearly overweight, his thick, bushy hair stuck out from under a wide-brimmed hat like half-shucked corn. An unkempt mustache wrapped around his face, meeting curly sideburns. Because of his size and shape, his clothes seemed rumpled and ill-fitting. But the big horse-pistol on his hip stuck out at an odd angle that Simms thought must be for an easy reach and quick draw. Despite his overall appearance, the doctor had no doubt the big man had the determination and experience to use that six-gun to back

64

up his friend no matter what the odds or situation.

Hollis assured the two men that if any new reward money came in he'd lock it in his office safe until he heard from Link. The four men briefly shook hands before Bonner and Bull exited the office, leaving Doctor Simms staring after them.

'This man, Bonner, seems a very unusual person. Don't you think so, Sheriff?'

Hollis pulled at his jaw, mulling the statement over. 'He's unusual all right. But something tells me he's going to end up dead one of these days and it won't be from old age, either. Anyone fool enough to take on five men like Shin's gang just to get a week's wages back, sooner or later has to end up with the cards dealt against him. It's just a matter of time.'

'Maybe,' Simms mused. 'Maybe not. I'm certain we haven't heard the last about Mr Bonner, or his big friend either.'

Link and Bull rode out of Arroyo Grande, cloaked in a growing reputation Bonner would never shed. Whether or not he sought the fame of a man with a fast gun-hand and the grit to use it, the die was cast. Wherever he went from that day forward, he was instantly perceived as too dangerous to get close to unless you needed the services of his special talents and would pay the price to attain them.

Riding northwest, Link considered where he and Tate might head for next. One thing he was certain of, it would not be another small cow-town like Mesquite or Arroyo Grande. Maybe, he thought, he could lose his identity in a bigger, bustling town where people filled the streets and every man was a stranger. The more he considered it, the more it seemed to make sense. Obscurity might offer the peace of mind he sought.

'How'd you like to see a town like Sacramento?' he suddenly asked Tate one morning as they were breaking camp before saddling up.

'Sacramento? That's an awful long ways from here. We'd have to push these horses for nearly a month. You sure about that? Neither of us have ever been there or anyplace even close. That's damn near to the ocean, ain't it?'

'No, not that far. We would have to get over the Sierra Nevada Mountains, but now the weather is right for it. Most of the snow should be gone. The big gold strike they made out there a couple of years ago should make a town like that grow fast. I need a change, Bull. I want to get away to someplace new. Maybe start a new life of some kind. Would you still ride with me if I headed that way?'

Tate realized Link's question was more than just a suggestion. He could tell from the tone of his voice he was serious about it. He hesitated before answering, thinking about his own future too. He'd always been comfortable as a working cowboy out in the open, sometimes a ranchhand and really a small-town man. A big city like Sacramento was none of that from what little he'd heard about it. He couldn't imagine himself being hemmed in like that. He tried to choose his words carefully. He didn't want to part company with Link. They'd been close friends through thick and thin since they were just kids. He figured they always would be. But Sacramento was asking too much.

'I don't know.' He slowly shook his head. 'I'm not sure a big town like that is for me. Too many people always crowding, shoving, pushing in around you. I don't like crowds. You know I've always been a country boy, don't you Link?'

'I do. That's why I'm asking you about it straight out now before I ride west. I'd like you to be with me. We've always been a solid team no matter what came up. You're like a brother I never had. Probably even better. You know that. I think we can make it work, but I need a change and want to try for it out there.'

'Why don't we try someplace closer to home? What about Denver? We could take a look at that. They say it's getting to be a big town too.'

'No.' Link shook his head. 'I want to go west for a while to someplace I've never been where no one knows me. If I stay in this country much longer there's going to be more killing. It follows me around like a dark cloud. Maybe I can change my luck out there.'

'Well, if you're that dead set on it I can't change your mind. I never figured on us splitting up. I guess all this sorta took me by surprise. I'll likely have to ride back home to Mountain Gate. Sacramento just ain't for me.'

'I understand. You know I'll miss not having you with me. I've gotten pretty used to it after all these years. If I ever hear from Hollis about any of that reward money, I'll let you know and send you your share. We both earned it.'

'I ain't worried about that. You just take care of yourself and watch your back. I won't be there to do it for you like you're used to. No tellin' what might be coming your way out there in a place like that.'

The two men locked hands and eyes, holding on hard for several seconds longer before Link flashed a quick smile, turning to mount up. Tate stood watching him go, his mind clouded with misgivings. He knew Link couldn't run from himself and his growing legacy of six-gun encounters, but there was nothing he could say or do about changing his mind. Sacramento was just a name in loose-talk saloons and the streets of small, wild western towns. He feared Link could be heading for more trouble there than he ever imagined, but couldn't stop him. The big man saddled up, taking one long look back as Bonner's image became smaller and smaller until lost in the distance. He couldn't help but wonder if he'd ever see Link again.

Bonner rode steadily west over the next two weeks until reaching the banks of the Humboldt River, following it across sage and alkali flats for another seven days until the mighty ramparts of the granite peaks of the Sierra Nevada range rose up in front of him. Somewhere over those tops, far down the other side lay the vast river valley and the town of Sacramento located at the confluence of two great rivers, the Sacramento and American. Reaching the first pine-studded foothills, Bonner followed a large river flowing out of the mountains past a big, oval-shaped lake starting up into thick timber. Remnants of last winter's snows lay colored and decaying under evergreens and hidden pockets of shade. In four more days he reached the high pass over the top, starting down the western slope. Late one afternoon nearly a week later, he reined to a halt. As far as the eye could see, a broad, flat valley stretched away both north and south with the silver glint of a wide, meandering river running through it. It could only be the five-hundred mile long Sacramento.

Bonner made camp that evening on the edge of the last foothills. When darkness cloaked the sky, he lit a small campfire to sit by and eat dinner, watching the distant glow of lights coming on like flitting fireflies that was Sacramento's night life. Tomorrow he'd ride in to see if the town was all he'd hoped it would be.

The steel shoes on Link's horse rang loudly off the

hard cobblestones as he rode down busy Front Street, toward the river landing called the Embarcadero. Everywhere around him people were busy going some-place in a rush. Three pigtailed Chinese men plodded down the sidewalk, engaged in whispered conversation, wearing strange, dress-like gowns above wooden clog shoes. Another group of rough-looking men wearing wide-brimmed hats, dirt-stained clothes and muddy boots, must be miners just in from the gold fields of the mother lode in the Sierra foothills east of town. Several conspicuous men maneuvered their way through the crowd, dressed in expensive clothes and coats, wearing shiny, high-topped hats of the wealthy. They escorted well-dressed ladies wearing expensive, embroidered shawls under fancy hats and fashionable carousels. Above the milling throng, tall, two-story buildings lined both sides of the street and he rode past the Eagle Theater with the evening bill-board propped out front announcing a new play just in from New York. Bonner sat back in the saddle, taking it all in, marveling at the strange mix of humanity. He could not help but wonder if he would find a place for himself in all this.

Farther along Front Street, he came to the riverfront landing where barges, tied up side by side were busy with sweaty men laboring to load and unload supplies, people, cattle and horses. The watery passage down the Sacramento River led all the way through delta marsh-lands, Grizzly Bay and eventually to another fast-growing city, San Francisco, where trade and supply houses fueled the river city all because of the Sierra gold strike. Men and women from around the world, speaking strange lan-guages, landed in the bay city, departing tall clipper ships to head inland, stopping at Sacramento first for supplies and directions. They'd spent life savings and every cent they owned for the chance to live out their dream of striking it rich, making millions, finding yellow iron.

After touring the town for another hour, Bonner decided to rent a room at the Hawthorn Hotel. The Hawthorn was not the fanciest he'd seen nor the most run down. He elected for something in the middle of town and a modest price to make his money stretch as far and as long as possible. The counter man eyed him curiously as he stepped through the foyer up to the counter, sliding his saddle bags on top. He'd seen men of every stripe and persuasion, but nothing quite like Link Bonner.

'Mister, if you don't mind me saying so, I'd guess you're new in town, right?'

Link nodded but did not answer.

'The reason I asked is you don't have to come and go here in the hotel or outside on the street with that six-shooter strapped on your hip. You might scare other guests, if you know what I mean?'

An uncomfortable few seconds of silence passed as the two men eyed each other.

'Don't get me wrong. I don't mean any disrespect, but you don't have to walk around town armed to the teeth.'

'Where I come from, just about every man who is a man, carries his hardware on him,' Link gave a short explanation.

'Well, Mister, this isn't where you came from. Sacramento means to be a civilized town even if it is still a little rough around the edges. We've got lawmen here to take care of trouble. You don't have to do it yourself. I'd suggest you put that hog-leg away like most everyone else does.'

'You have someone to take my horse to a livery stable?'

70

Link ignored the suggestion.

'I've got a boy does chores for me. That will cost another two dollars, though.'

Link pushed the money across the counter after signing in, choosing a room on the second floor facing the street. He wanted to be able to stand at a window, watching the throng of people passing below, still trying to get a feel for this new city. Once upstairs in the room he closed and locked the door, looking around at its bare necessities; an old brass bed sagged against one wall opposite and a well-worn dresser with a small mirror atop it. A wash basin half-filled with water sat on top of the dresser. A rickety chair sat in one corner facing the window. The floor was bare wood with one small rug frayed at the edges next to the bed. An enameled bed pan peeked out from under the frame. Link walked to the bed, testing it, laying down. He sank so deep in the worn-out springs, he had to roll to get back out, wondering if he could actually sleep in such a contraption. Sitting down on the edge, he thought about his strained conversation with the counterman about openly carrying his six-gun. He'd belt-worn a pistol since he was a teenager. Going without it now would be like walking out in the street half dressed. He wasn't certain he could do that, city or no city.

Late that afternoon Bonner went back downstairs. Outside, the sun was just sinking behind tall buildings as he started down the street, caught up in a crowd of people. He was swept by store-fronts selling all manner of items anyone could want, but one on the next block caught his eye, because of the display of guns behind the big, glass window. He exited the throng, stepping inside. George Latrell, the shop owner, was sitting at a small table, bent over the pieces of a stripped-down revolver. The sound of hard-soled boots across the floor broke his concentration. He came to his feet, glasses perched on the end of his nose, studying his new customer.

'What can I do for you?' He eyed tall, dark-haired Bonner, noting his unusual dress, wide-brimmed hat and high-topped boots.

'I saw some odd-looking pistols in your window. One smaller one looked like it came with leather straps that buckled onto a holster. I've never seen one quite like that before.'

Latrell walked to the display, lifting the little gun and holster out, turning back to Bonner. 'Is this it?' Link nodded.

'These are called belly guns.'

'Belly guns?'

'Yes. They're made to carry out of sight under a coat or jacket about waist-high. Some have a leather harness like this one, to keep the holster right where you want it. This one is a Remington .41 caliber double-barrel derringer. It's wicked at short range. Gentlemen of the night go for them.'

'What kind of gentleman is that?'

'I'd say card players, gamblers, drinkers, boozers and trouble-makers too, anyone who wants a weapon to back them up but doesn't want to show it. You don't look much like any of them to me, though.'

'Is that why they call them belly guns?'

'I imagine so. Maybe it's also because you carry them belly-high, or if you have a disagreement at a card table, you can put two bullets into someone under the table belly-high. Either way, it's a stomachache you won't get over.'

'I'd like to try one on for size. The one with the harness and holster, and box of cartridges too. I don't think I want any pistol just stuck down my pants.'

'I'd call that a wise decision.' Latrell nodded.

Back in his hotel room, Link lit the coal-oil lamp on the mirror stand. Taking off his jacket he slipped into the leather harness, buckling and adjusting it against his shirt. Sliding the Remington into the holster, he went to the mirror, putting his jacket back on. He moved the holster slightly left out of sight, satisfied it could not be seen, before going back downstairs to take in the sights and sounds of his first night in Sacramento.

Card rooms, saloons and gambling houses were already loud with the sound of customers enjoying another night on the town. Two blocks down the street around a corner, he came to a gambling house called the Red Dragon's Den. Strange aromas drifted from inside, even past closed double doors. He pushed them open to the loud mix of talk and laughter. A sweet, blue smoke permeated a big room lit with lanterns near each gambling table crowded with wagering men. The unusual smell came from incense burning in small trays, each one emitting a different fragrance. Link immediately noticed many Chinese playing at the tables, especially the Faro tables. American Poker, Mexican Monte and several roulette wheels were also in play. One table seemed to draw the most customers and the loudest talk. He moved through the crowd toward it, instantly seeing why.

A stunningly-beautiful Mexican woman named Lola Montenegro was dealing American Poker. Her long, jet-black hair hung in curls down to her shoulders. Dark, flashing eyes were accentuated by full lips painted fiery red. Her expensive, sequined gown was cut daringly low, exposing cleavage of shapely breasts and high above the knee, revealing perfectly sculptured legs ending in lace-up boots. When Lola's lips parted in a smile, bright, white teeth framed the lovely shade of her smooth, sepia-brown skin. Men at her table were not only betting large sums of money on each hand, but also tipping her lavishly, win, lose or draw, to gain her attention and favor. Bonner edged closer, fascinated to watch her work through each deal, cajoling men to bet even higher stakes. She was a consummate professional, using every element of her womanly ways to keep the game moving at a fast pace as money piled up on the table, while she won most hands.

As one man playing in front of Link, finally ran out of money, he stood to leave his chair. Without missing a beat, Lola tossed him a ten-dollar gold piece from her pile of cash. 'Don't go home broke again tonight sweetie, or your wife will toss you out in the alley,' she demurred, the circle of men at the table laughing out loud at her bold pronouncement, while the poor man slunk off into the crowd, red faced and embarrassed. She glanced up at Link.

'There's an empty seat. You want to try your luck, sweetie?' she challenged him.

'No.' He shook his head. 'I don't gamble on cards. It's a bad habit I don't need any more of.'

'Then why are you here watching me?'

'I'm new in town, just looking things over.'

'Well, you've gotten an eye full of me. What do you think about that, Mr New In Town?'

Link stared back, realizing she was trying to embarrass him just as she'd done the man who'd left. A small smile lit his lips. He wasn't going to give her that chance. If it was a game she wanted to play, he'd deal himself in on this one.

'I was watching you because I think you like the attention you get from all these suckers while you clean them out. It's quite an act. You must have had a lot of practice at it in here.'

'Hey, wait a minute, cowboy,' a man sitting at the far end of the table broke in. 'You can't insult Miss Montenegro like that. Who in hell do you think you are, come walking in here shooting off your mouth?'

Link turned to the big, well-dressed man, still in his seat, eyeing him a moment. 'No one's talking to you. Mind your own business,' he shot back, the look in his eyes made it clear he meant every word of it.

'I'm just saying . . .'

'I'm telling you to keep it to yourself, or I'll make you eat your words.'

A sudden quiet came over the table, each man in his seat casting furtive glances at other players all ready to quickly vacate their chairs if it went any further. Lola realized it was too explosive, not to mention bad for business. She quickly broke in to end it.

'Listen, you two. Just shut up and buy me a drink. I'm here to deal poker, not start trouble and lose my job. Go on J.J., get me a drink from the bar. I'll hold your seat,' she ordered the man in fancy clothes.

J.J. Campbell slowly pushed back from his chair, getting up still mumbling to himself under his breath, disappearing into the crowd, heading for the bar, while Lola turned her attention back to Link.

'You do like to stir things up, don't you Mr . . . do you have a name?'

'It's Bonner, Link Bonner.'

'Well, Mr Link Bonner with the steely eyes, are you in or out now that you've caused all this excitement?'

75

'I said I don't play cards. You'll have to deal me out.' He pushed a five-dollar gold piece across the table. 'This is for the lesson.'

'What lesson?' Lola stared back, for once without a fast follow-up.

'The lesson how you control this rowdy bunch in here and make them like it. It was something to watch. I've never seen anyone else do it quite like that before.'

Link flashed a quick smile before turning away from the table into the crowd as her eyes followed him until John Jenkins Campbell came back to the table with her drink.

'Let's play cards.' One of the men broke the tense atmosphere. She took one long sip at the glass before beginning a new shuffle.

CHAPTER SIX

There was no closing time at the Red Dragon's Den, but the crowd began to thin out well past midnight. Link was sitting at the bar sipping a whiskey, when Lola came up behind him.

'Mind if I sit down, Mr Link Bonner?'

'It's your place. You can do anything you want, but I'll stand you a drink if you'd like one?' He turned, facing her, pulling the bar stool out.

'Mack, a glass of sweet wine for me,' she ordered the bartender.

'Right away, ma'am.' He nodded.

'You do like to order people around, don't you?' Link tried to keep it light.

'I make the Red Dragon fifteen-thousand dollars a week at my one table. That's a big pile of cash even after I get my share. Ming Too, who owns this place, knows it. He counts every single dollar. When I want something, I expect to get it. But that's not why I came over here.'

'I thought you might want to teach me how to play poker.' Link couldn't help needling her a little bit more.

'No, I'm not kidding about this and neither should you. You made yourself the wrong enemy with J.J. Campbell earlier tonight at my table. He's got a lot of money and influence in town. He's not going to forget you called him out and embarrassed him in front of everyone. No one else dares do that to him.'

'Then he should have stood up and made his play, if he's man enough.'

'No, you don't understand. Double J doesn't operate that way. He never gets his hands dirty because he doesn't have to. He has other men do that for him. He won't forget you. I'm warning you. You'd better watch yourself.'

'So, what makes him such a big man?'

'He owns most of the river barges down at the Embarcadero, and half interest in a big paddle-wheeler called the "American Queen". It hauls passengers and freight from San Francisco up here twice a week. Some say he's even going to run for mayor of Sacramento. If he does, he'll probably win. Steer clear of him if you know what's good for you. You are smart enough to understand what I'm saying, aren't you, Mr Link Bonner?'

He stared back hard at Lola for several moments before answering. When he did, he caught her completely by surprise.

'Tell you what, Miss Montenegro. You're a betting woman. You want to make a little bet with me, and I don't mean on that card table of yours either?'

She paused, wondering what he was up to now. 'What kind of bet would that be?'

'You stop calling me Mr Bonner, and I'll stop calling you Miss Montenegro. You up for that, Lola?'

She couldn't suppress a tiny smile of awe and even a little bit of respect for this strange man who had walked into the Red Dragon's Den, creating a small furor at her table without turning a card or betting a single dollar.

'All right Mr . . . Link,' she caught herself, extending her hand filled with jeweled rings on most fingers. 'I'll take your bet for now and see how it goes. Now I've got to get back to my table. Before I go, do you mind me asking what do you do for a living?'

'Right now, nothing. I'm going to have to start looking pretty quick, though.'

'I see. Well, enjoy your drink. I hope you find something that matches your talents. You obviously have some, don't you?'

'That's been said.' Link smiled, holding her hand a moment longer before letting go. Lola Montenegro fascinated him. There was no doubt about that. He'd never encountered a woman so independent and sure of herself. When she was at her table, dealing cards, she ruled that world completely. He could not help but admire her for that and the way she carried herself at work or not, as she'd just shown him. He'd have to keep his emotions in check for sure with this dazzling lady.

For the next several nights Link purposely stayed out of the Red Dragon's Den, even though he thought more than once about going back. He did want to see Lola again, but not make it obvious. During days he walked the streets of town looking for work.

Living in Sacramento was outrageously expensive. His small reserve of cash from Arroyo Grande was running dangerously low, and fast. The jobs he did find were back-breaking, menial labor quickly snapped up by men even more desperate than him to turn a dollar. He told himself he was better than that even if he had to leave Sacramento to survive. At the end of that week he walked back into the Red Dragon's Den, as evening gamblers were just hitting their stride. The place was loud with laughter and that sweet smell of incense permeating the room. Across the room Lola's table was busy with poker players. She flashed her alluring smile, keeping everyone betting big and the conversation lively. Glancing up she saw Link moving through the crowd toward her. She'd looked for him most of that week, glad he finally showed up. He stopped behind the seated players, nodding a quick smile of hello. Reaching into the top of her blouse, she pulled out a folded piece of paper, handing it to him without saying a word, continuing her fast-paced conversation with players. Link stepped back, unfolding the note and reading it.

'Ming Too wants to talk to you. See Mack at the bar.'

Link looked up, wondering what all this was about. She only gave him a quick glance before nodding at the bar across the room. Folding the note, he started for the busy counter. Mack was serving a line of men at the far end when he reached the bar so he waited for him to come down his way. When he did, he handed the barkeep the note.

'Lola says Ming Too wants to see me. How do I find him?'

Mack stared back, wondering if this was some kind of joke. No one saw the elusive, Chinese owner. 'You sure about this?' he questioned.

'Lola gave it to me. I didn't make it up.'

'OK,' he shrugged. 'You cross the room over to that hallway and walk down to the end. There's a locked door there. Knock on it and see if someone answers. If he does, you give them this note real quick before he throws you out in the alley. Good luck with it. Ming never talks to visitors. You get my drift?'

Bonner crossed the noisy room and down the dark hallway. A heavy, wooden door at the end had strange oriental symbols written across the front. He knocked loudly three times. Minutes passed without an answer. He tried again. This time the lock clicked and the door opened, with a huge Chinese man filling the doorway nearly top to bottom, glaring down on him.

'What . . . you . . . want?' he growled in a threatening tone. Link handed him Lola's note. He read it before answering, 'You . . . wait . . . here.' The door slammed shut.

Bonner stood wondering what all this was about. Several more minutes passed before the door opened again. The giant Asian stepped out, pushing Link up against the wall, searching him for weapons. Finding the derringer and holster, he stripped them off. Clamping a giant hand on Link's shoulder, he led him inside through another room to a second door. Knocking once, he slowly opened the door, pushing Link in ahead of him. A large, fat Chinese man sat, wearing a simple but brilliantly-colored red robe. Pillows were scattered across the floor, the smell of incense nearly overpowering. His small eyes did not blink, surveying his visitor. A skimpy mustache circled his mouth, ending in a long, thin beard over a double chin. Next to him sat two pretty young oriental girls dressed in bright, multi-colored silk gowns, their feet adorned in white, cloth-wrapped, wooden clogs. The bodyguard handed Ming Too Bonner's derringer and holster, uttering a few brief words in Chinese. Ming Too turned the weapon in his hands. A flicker of a smile played across his broad face.

'You Americans are a crafty people,' he said in perfect English, the two concubines at his side giggling their approval. 'Do you really think this little pop-gun of yours would protect you from the ravages of Sacramento at night?'

'It's a .41 Remington. That's enough caliber to get any man's attention. Carrying my .45 belt gun around seemed to upset people, so I purchased this one.'

'I see.' Ming Too pursed his lips. 'Do you know why I've sent for you?'

'I do not. Lola's note didn't say.'

'Then let me carefully explain something to you Mr Bonner. The Red Dragon's Den sees many people from all over the world; white, black, Asians and others. If you have been observant, you should also have seen that many who come here to gamble and drink are of Asian descent. A few drink too much and gamble too much. They become troublesome. I have Loy here to handle people of my skin color. But I also have many Americans too, just like you. They can become, shall we say belligerent, when a Chinese man has to remove them. They think yellow people are below their race, and that can cause further trouble even though they drink my liquor and gamble their money here. I have been thinking about hiring a white man to take care of men like that. Miss Montenegro knew this and suggested your name to me for the job. She tells me you are a man of principle and purpose, who does not back down in the face of adversity. Are you such a man, Mr Bonner?'

The sudden offer of a job like this took Link by complete surprise. It required a moment for him to think it through. He needed a good-paying job and hadn't found one. Something like this never crossed his mind before. He answered more out of the need to say something, instead of standing there speechless.

'What does this job of yours pay?'

'Ah, you Americans. Always thinking of money.' Ming shook his head, the girls giggling dutifully on cue. 'The pay is two-hundred dollars a week. I pay every Sunday night, in gold and silver coin. No paper money. Now what is your answer, Mr Bonner?'

'Do I have a free hand to do as I please?'

'You do. Only don't shoot anyone with your little gun unless it's out in the alley. Killing and blood disrupts the gambling tables. I expect you to be discreet about any Americans that might get out of hand, and one other thing. Remember I have Loy here, to take care of Asians. Your job is to handle the whites. Now do we clearly understand each other, Mr Bonner?'

'We do. When do you want me to start?'

'When Loy takes you back into the gambling room, you'll be in my employ. Don't let Miss Montenegro down. She obviously thinks you are the man for the job or she wouldn't have gone out of her way to suggest you.'

'I won't let her down or you either.'

'Good. Now go to work, and remember – no shooting or blood inside my establishment.'

Back in the main room, the door to Ming Too's mysterious world closed behind Link Bonner. Across the crowd he could see Lola dealing at her table, with a circle of men filling every seat opposite her as usual. She'd saved his neck suggesting Ming Too hire him. He wondered if she really knew how near broke he was and how badly he needed a good-paying job. He was still unsure why she'd gone out of her way in the first place. Reaching her table, he silently mouthed the words, 'thank you.' Lola flashed a fleeting smile but did not speak. J.J. Campbell, sitting his usual chair in last spot, saw their brief exchange. His intense dislike of Bonner suddenly boiled to the surface again.

'Just deal the cards, Lola. Save the smiles for men here at the table, spending their money. Not the gallery who can't afford to sit down and play.'

Bonner felt the heat of anger quickly rise in his face, but he knew he had to temper it instead of yanking Campbell to his feet. He was now an employee of Ming Too, and his new boss made it clear he wanted no violence inside his gambling hall, if possible. Instead, Link moved around the players until he stood over Campbell. Leaning down he looked him in the eye only inches away, talking in a low, controlled tone just loud enough that others at the table could hear him.

'There isn't enough whiskey in this room to give you the backbone you need to stand up and take what you've got coming to you man to man. So just sit there and keep your big mouth shut or I'll haul you out of here by the scruff of your neck. I'm now employed here to remove trouble-makers like you.'

J.J. Campbell jerked back in his chair, wide-eyed with fear. 'What do you mean, you work here? Since when?'

'Since tonight. So watch that big mouth of yours or I'll make you my first customer.'

'Don't, Link!' Lola's voice was high-pitched with concern. 'Both of you calm down. This is a gambling house, not a cock-fighting ring. J.J., shut up and play your cards. Link, I can handle him. Let it go. He doesn't mean anything by it. Please don't take this any further.'

'All right, Lola. You better be able to or I will, either in here or outside on the street.'

The night shift for dealers ended at midnight when new dealers came on, playing until dawn. Link spent the remainder of that evening moving around the big room, watching other players and games, familiarizing himself with the entire operation. His shift started at eight each night, running until four a.m. About midnight, he had the chance to take a short break and did so this first night sitting at the bar, ordering just one whiskey while keeping an eye on the room and everyone in it.

'I see you're still here,' Mack the bartender said, coming up. 'I'm glad you didn't end up with Loy throwing you out in the alley. Everything must have worked out all right, huh?'

'It did. I'm now on the payroll.'

'Are you kidding me?'

'No, I'm not. Ming Too hired me to keep this place peaceable. That's what I mean to do starting tonight.'

'So, you're the new enforcer, huh? Ming hired another man to do that sometime back. He was a big man physically, bigger than you. One night after a couple of weeks he didn't show up for work. They found what was left of him floating face down in the river ten miles downstream. He was only fish food by then. He must have rubbed someone in here the wrong way. Never found out who it was.'

'I don't intend to do any swimming. Now how about that whiskey?'

Lola waited all evening to hear about Link's hiring. When her shift ended at midnight, she came to the bar where he was sitting.

'So, you got the job. Good for you.' She slid onto the stool next to him.

'I did, and I have you to thank for it. I was just about ready to pack up and leave this town. It's an expensive place to live if you're not making good money.'

'I thought you might end up losing your job over Double J this first night. You can't let anyone get to you like that. You'll have to learn to hold your temper.'

'That's something not easy for me to do. I've never had to before. When someone crosses the line with me, I've always taken care of it.'

'Maybe where you came from that's the way you did things, but not here, at least not working for Ming Too. You've got a good job I think you're well suited for. Don't throw it away over nothing. By the way, where did you come from? I've never seen you in here before and sooner or later just about everyone in Sacramento comes in here for something.'

'I came from no place you ever heard of. Besides, it's not important.'

She tossed her head back with a small laugh. 'Is it some kind of a secret all of a sudden?'

'Maybe. I came to Sacramento to change some things in my life, trying to outrun my past. I'm not sure yet if that will work either.'

'Change from what? I'd like to know if you'll tell me.'

He looked away from her for a moment, an almost inaudible sigh of exasperation passing his lips. Why was she so insistent? He already knew he found Lola more than fascinating, but explaining his life and what he'd done with a six-gun might change all that. Could he trust someone he'd only just met, with such personal things? He looked back at her as she smiled expectantly.

'I will tell you some of it if you'll let it go and not bring it up again.'

'Of course I will if that's the way you want it. I'm just curious about you, Link. You're not like most men that come in here. I saw that right off.'

'That's the way I want it. I've had a lot of different jobs and moved around a good deal too. But no matter where I went, it always ended up in gun play for one reason or another. I didn't go looking for it; it always seemed to follow me. I thought coming here to a big town with lots of people might end it. I'd get lost in the crowd.'

'You mean men were killed because of you?'

'That's what I mean. I'm still here. They're not. I've been a gun-hand for most of my adult life. I'm beginning to think that's the way I'll spend the rest of it. Have you ever heard the saying "live by the gun, die by the gun"?'

'Yes, I have.'

'That's what I was trying to change, coming here. And now I work for Ming Too, with orders that might lead right back to pistol work again and getting paid for it. He doesn't mind what I have to do as long as it's outside. Doesn't sound like much has changed, does it?'

Lola realized she had to change the subject. It made both her and Link uncomfortable. 'Listen, I'm off now. Would you like to escort a lady home? We could relax, forget about work, and have a glass of sweet wine. I don't go to bed until dawn anyway. Now you're on the same hours too.'

He stared back into those alluring eyes of hers. Was there a hint of something more than a glass of wine and idle conversation? There was only one way to find out.

'Yes, I'd like that. Going back to my room at the

Hawthorn isn't exactly what I'd call home.'

'You're staying there? It's kind of run down, isn't it? You can do better than that.'

'Yes, now that I have a good-paying job, I can.'

'Maybe on your day off we can find something else you'd like better? I know this town and everything in it.'

Outside the Red Dragon's Den, Lola and Link stopped for a moment, watching the shadowy figures of men and women of the night still passing up and down the thoroughfare. He noticed Lola looking up the street until she stepped forward off the curb, raising her hand as a horse-drawn carriage with an older man at the reins, pulled to a stop.

'What are you doing?' Link questioned.

'I'm taking a carriage home. I live outside of town several miles on the road close to the American River. If I lived in town I'd never get a night's rest. I like the privacy out there away from my job.'

'Eve'nen', Miss Montenegro. You want a ride home as usual?'

'I do, Sam.'

The driver eyed Bonner but made no remark. 'I figured you might be off work about now. That's why I stayed close to this block so I could see if you came out.'

'You figured right. Let's go home, Sam.'

The carriage clattered down cobblestone streets until leaving town and the glow of lamplight far behind. Out in the country the horse pulled at a steady, wheel-spinning trot, while overhead a black-velvet sky studded with a billion blazing stars lit the land in eerie star glow. Lola leaned back in the seat, closing her eyes, feeling the cool wind across her face. Link studied her, almost certain he could see a small smile crease ruby-red lips. He did not say a word to violate the peaceful moment. Instead, he leaned back too, never taking his eyes off this strange, strikingly-beautiful, unpredictable woman who had befriended him. What other surprises lay ahead, he wondered.

CHAPTER SEVEN

The carriage pulled to a squeaky stop in front of Lola's home surrounded by a copse of huge, shadowed oak trees. She opened her small, jeweled purse, paying Sam, before she and Link stepped down.

'Thank you, Miss Montenegro.' The driver tipped his hat. 'I'll be looking for you tomorrow night again after work.'

'Not tomorrow, Sam. I've got the day off.'

'Oh, all right, ma'am. Then the night after that, if you'd like.'

'That would be fine. Goodnight, Sam. Say hello to your miss's for me. And thanks for the ride.'

Sam pulled the wagon around, starting back toward the distant glow of Sacramento, slowly disappearing into the night to the fading clop of hoof beats. Lola and Link stood a moment watching it go.

'Let's get inside and start a fire,' she urged, wrapping her arm around his. 'It's not winter yet, but I love a fire even when the night's just get a little cool like this. Don't you?'

'Yes, I do. As long as I don't have to chop the wood for it,' he kidded.

Inside the adobe-walled home Lola lit a pair of lamps,

illuminating a large, central room. Fancy Mexican sombreros hung from the wall like expensive paintings and coarse, woven, multi-colored wool rugs carpeted the red tile floor. She pointed to the fireplace. 'Why don't you get a fire going while I change into something more comfortable? Then I'll get our drinks.'

Link already had a good fire crackling to life when she came back into the room, wearing a full-length, dark-blue evening robe that swept the floor when she walked. She looked even more breathtakingly stunning than before. Link's long stare instantly got her attention.

'Haven't you ever seen a lady in her evening robe before?' she smiled.

'I've seen my share. But none of them were quite as pretty as you.'

'Thank you, Link. That compliment will get you a glass of sweet wine.'

Lola poured two glasses from a new bottle, handing Link one then sat on the couch, taking a pencil-thin, dark-colored cigarillo from a ten-pack wrapped in black paper. Lighting it she sipped at the glass as the two began talking about their pasts, good times and bad. Link was especially keen to learn how Lola ended up in Sacramento of all places, to eventually become the toast of the gambling crowd and many others in town as well.

'My mother, father and I were from Ensenada, in Mexico. We lived in the hills above the bay. He was a fisherman. As a little girl I used to run down to the beach and play, waiting for him to come back in. My mother was never very well. She suffered from many things and we had little money to live on. When gold was discovered here, my father told us we were all moving north. He thought he would become rich digging for yellow iron. It's the same thing that still drives many men mad today. But the only luck we had was all bad. My mother died after only one year living here. A gringo doctor told us it was consumption. After that my father was away a lot as I grew up. I was fifteen by then and worked at any job I could find to support myself. One day I was given a message that my father had died someplace up in the mining hills. It did not say how or exactly where. Only that he was *muerto sin vida*. I decided then, I would never live poorly again. I found salvation in a simple deck of cards while I was working at Ming Too's, cooking and cleaning up. I learned poker and the odds of the game from top to bottom. Ming finally gave me a table to try me out. I became good at the game, and also understood the looks I got from men who came back again and again each night to my table. I haven't lived poorly in a long time, Link. And I have no intention of ever having to again.'

'I'd say you've done pretty well for yourself in this wide-open town.'

'I have the top table at Ming's. And I plan to keep it that way.'

'Do you mind me asking you something more personal?'

She hesitated before answering, wondering what. 'Ask me first, and I'll tell you if I do.'

'What's your connection to this blow-hard, Campbell? He spends just about every night at your table. Is he your boyfriend or something? He doesn't look like he's making any money doing it.'

'Double J is a man who thinks he can buy anything he wants, including people, if he just spends enough money. You're right. He's not especially good at poker, but he doesn't care and tips well.'

'Are you saying he's been trying to buy your affections?'

'Yes, and sometimes I let him think someday he might, even though that will never happen. As I told you before, he's someone not to make an enemy of. He has powerful friends all over Sacramento, in politics and business. It's best you just try to ignore him at the club. Most men at my table would never cross him as you have. You're the exception, and he won't forget it. You have to be more careful.'

'I can handle myself, Lola. I always have.'

'Yes, I saw that in you. But you are only one man. And one man against three or four is no match you can win. Not even for you, Link. We've been up a long time talking. I'm getting tired and it will soon be dawn. I think it's best we both get some sleep, don't you?'

'Sure. Where are . . . we sleeping?' He took the chance to include them both.

'We, aren't sleeping anywhere. You're sleeping out here on the couch. Blankets are over on the chair. I'm sleeping in my bedroom, and don't wake me up. I keep a pistol on the night-stand next to my bed for unwanted visitors. I like you a lot Link, but not that much. At least not yet. Now, good night.'

She got up, leaning down, kissing him lightly on the cheek. He watched every step she took across the room until closing the bedroom door behind her, hearing the lock click shut. Link stretched out on the couch, smiling to himself. This woman Lola Montenegro, was unlike anyone he'd ever met before. He wondered if there would be other nights spent at the adobe-walled house near the rushing American River, and if they'd end up any differently.

The nighttime carriage rides to Lola's home became a regular event in the following weeks leading to months.

Link no longer slept on the couch, as he and Lola realized there was more to them spending time together than just a curious fascination with each other. Both inexorably began to fall deeply in love, despite their efforts not to let things get that serious.

Fall then winter came to the Sacramento Valley with torrents of seasonal rain driven by hurricane winds rushing in over coastal mountains to the west. The Sacramento and American Rivers, swollen and muddy-brown, climbed their banks, going over the top, flooding much of the town. Businesses closed, some for good. Men waded the streets while others rowed from block to block, but the Red Dragon's Den stayed open regardless of the misery affecting most of the town. It still rang with the talk and laughter of gamblers, drinkers and prospectors betting their last dollar to beat the odds and win enough money for one more grub-stake in the golden foothills and mountains east of town.

J.J. Campbell sat in his usual seat at Lola's poker table. Even though she and Link tried to keep their growing affection for each other a secret when at work, it was a secret that could not last. Eventually most customers and workers in Ming Too's became aware of it. When Campbell finally realized he'd lost any chance he thought he had to win Lola's affections, and especially to a man he already hated, it turned into serious trouble at her gambling table on more than one occasion. Her quick smiles, then out-right pleading with him not to make a scene, fell on deaf ears. Campbell was used to getting what he wanted one way or the other. It drove him recklessly wild that he could not. He argued about card play especially when he lost, accusing Lola of palming some bets or dealing off the bottom of the deck. One Saturday night it all finally spilled over.

Link was across the room when he heard a loud commotion at Lola's table. He immediately pushed his way through the crowd of men up to the circle of poker players. One look at Lola's face was all it took to see she was desperate for help. Campbell had his back to Link as he loudly berated Lola about losing what he was certain was one of his rare winning hands.

'I had three aces!' he shouted, red faced, getting to his feet, shaking his cards in her face. 'There's no way in hell you could have naturally drawn two cards to a heart flush against me without cheating!'

Link quickly moved behind Campbell, grabbing him by the shoulder, spinning him around. 'Take your money off the table, and get out of here now while you can,' he ordered, trying to control his own rising temper.

'You go to hell, Bonner. I could buy a drifter like you ten times over and still have change left. This game is rigged. I've known it for a long time. I want the money in that pot, and I want it right now!'

'Lola, how much did this loud-mouth loser bet?' Link asked, as more men began crowding in around the table, wondering what all the shouting was about.

'He . . . had three-hundred.' She nodded toward the pile of coins and paper money in the middle of the table.

'Count out his bet,' Link ordered.

She did so quickly, handing him the three-hundred. Link shoved the bills into Campbell's jacket pocket. 'Now get out of here and don't came back until you can act like a gentleman, instead of a sore-nosed loser.'

Campbell exploded, taking a wild swing at Link, only grazing his shoulder as he ducked under it. He came back up, sending a crashing right hand under J.J.'s jaw, dropping him onto the floor like a sack of wheat, nearly unconscious, thrashing around trying to regain his feet. Before he could, Link reached down, dragging him upright with both hands, marching the wobbly-legged man towards the front door. Shoving Campbell outside, he kicked him hard in the seat of his pants, sending him sprawling face-first with a splash into the scum of icy water, mud and small debris flooding the street.

'You come back in here again and start trouble, you'll wish you were never born,' Link threatened as Campbell struggled up to his knees, dripping wet and filthy, spitting water.

'You . . . just signed . . . your own death warrant. I'll . . . see to it!' he screamed, gasping for breath.

A week had passed since the humiliating beating taken by Campbell at the hands of Link Bonner. He'd bided his time nursing a swollen jaw and fat lip, plotting how he'd get even. He'd also stayed out of the Red Dragon's Den. Instead, this night he walked through dark streets toward the Embarcadero where his river barges were tied up at the boat dock, riding the gurgle of an unrelenting current. The waterfront was completely deserted except for a dim light behind curtains in a small shack at the far end. Reaching it he put his ear to the door. Inside he could hear men talking in low tones. He knocked three times in a spaced-out rhythm. The talking suddenly stopped followed by a rustle of activity, before the door opened just a crack. A rough-looking, heavily-bearded man peeked out, lifting a lantern.

'Oh, it's you, boss. Can't be too careful these days about who's roaming around at night down here. Know what I mean?'

Campbell didn't answer, stepping inside. Three other

men stood around a table. Two half-empty bottles of whiskey were surrounded by scattered coins and playing cards. For the first time everyone got a good look at their boss.

'Hey, what happened to you? You look all busted up,' one man said.

'Never mind what happened to me. I've got a job for you four and I want it done right, understand? There can't be any slip-ups. There's a new man working at the Red Dragon's Den, named Link Bonner. He's supposed to be the law in the place. He's gotten too big for his boots, and I want him removed the same way you did Vince Towrey, the last one Ming hired for the same job. You be at the Red Dragon's Den next Friday night at three o'clock. I'll be at my usual poker table, with Lola Montenegro. When Bonner comes over I'll point him out to you. His shift ends at four a.m. When he comes outside it will still be dark, so be absolutely certain you've got the right man. I want him eliminated quickly. Dump him in the river like before. If you have any questions, let's get them over with right now.'

'You want us to use knives or guns?' the bearded man asked.

'Use pistols, and be certain you put plenty of lead into him. I want him stone-cold dead in the street. You do this right and I'll stake all of you to a vacation in San Francisco on the American Queen for a few days while things cool down. Do I make myself clear?'

'We'll be there at three sharp,' the bearded man promised.

Lola had looked for Campbell every night since Link had unceremoniously thrown him out in the street. The first few nights she was nervous he'd show up again to make more trouble. When he had not by later that week, she knew him well enough to worry he was working on a scheme to get even with Link. During her break from the poker table she warned Link about her fears.

'You know J.J. hasn't been in here all week, don't you?'

'Yes, I do. I've been looking for him too.'

'He's not going to let what you did to him go unanswered. I know him well enough to be sure of that. You embarrassed him in front of everyone. He won't forget it. I want you to be careful both in here and outside on the street. You and I have found something very special between us. I don't want anything to change that, Link. If J.J. does show up, promise me you won't make an issue of it again. You and I aren't going to work here forever. Maybe someday we will both want to move away from here and have a life of our own together. I've known many men before but no one like you. I've never said that to any man before. I hope you feel the same way about it.'

'I do, Lola. You're special to me too.' He clutched her hand, surprised at her sudden admission. 'Don't worry. I won't make any trouble as long as he doesn't start it again. I have my job here to think about too, just like you.'

'I cannot have what happened in here repeated. That won't work out well for either of us, especially for future plans we make.'

'I don't think he'll do something like that again. He knows he can't get away with it in here because I won't stand for it. Now stop worrying about it.'

She smiled, pursing her lips in a silent kiss. 'We'll go home to my place after work, won't we? And this Sunday I think it's time you left the Thornton and moved your things in with me.'

'You bet I will, hon. I'd like nothing better.'

Friday night's heaviest gambling hours were nearly over

when J.J. Campbell walked through the front door of the Red Dragon's Den, immediately making his way across the room to Lola's table. When she saw him, her heart skipped a beat with fear for two reasons. First, another man was sitting in his usual seat, and second, what he might do after the humiliating beating Link had given him. When he reached the table, he walked up to the stranger in his chair, glaring down on him.

'You're in my chair. Get out of it!'

The startled man looked up, starting to put up an argument until Lola quickly broke in before another disastrous scene took place. 'Please, Mr Bryson. You are sitting in J.J.'s seat, and he's paid plenty for it.' She pushed a ten-dollar gold coin across the table to him with a quick smile. 'There's another seat at the end of the table. Here's a little gift for being a sweetheart about moving.'

Bryson slowly got to his feet, grumbling under his breath, scooping up his money, moving along. Campbell immediately sat down. Opening a thick, leather wallet, he laid out five one-hundred dollar bills before glancing up at Lola with an icy stare.

'It's nice to see you again, J.J.. I hope you've calmed down by now and won't make a scene over what happened last time you were in here.'

He answered with just three words. 'Deal the cards.'

Campbell lost the first hand and was well on his way to doing the same with the second when his four men stepped through the front door. They looked around the room a moment before seeing him, starting for Lola's poker table. Coming up behind their boss, one man leaned down whispering something. Campbell turned, nodding but did not answer.

Lola saw the quick exchange, eyeing the four. She saw a

lot of faces come and go in Ming Too's, and always made it a point to try and remember each one, who they were and how they played their cards. It was part of her overall winning strategy to do so. These four rough-looking men were not regulars, but obviously they knew Campbell well enough to come over and make their presence known. She wondered why, deciding to try and find out in her own way.

'You gentlemen can sit in. My table is open with two more seats,' she offered, motioning at the empty chairs, looking each one of them over carefully.

The heavily-bearded man moved uneasily at being called out so openly. 'We . . . I mean I ain't playing.' He quickly corrected himself.

'What about you other three?' Lola quickly countered. 'You're here, why not enjoy yourself and try to win a little money if you can?'

'Lola, just deal the damn cards and forget about it!' J.J. broke in, the irritation in his loud voice obvious, carrying across the partially-filled room.

Bonner turned around, recognizing Campbell's whiney protest, immediately starting for Lola's table as she dealt out the cards. Coming up behind the players he stopped right in back of J.J.'s chair, glancing across at Lola. She did a quick, barely perceptible head shake warning him not to start anything. Campbell felt his presence too. Twisting in his chair, he looked up.

'Well, if it isn't Link Bonner, Lola's new boyfriend,' he mocked. 'You still trying to make a living throwing paying customers out of here, or did Ming Too tell you he's already losing money on you?'

The four men looked Link up and down. They had their mark. Campbell saw it too, satisfied he'd pointed

Link out, before turning back to his cards. 'Get lost, Bonner. I'm not going to give you an excuse for trying to throw me out again.'

Lola saw Link's temper building, quickly deciding to step in before it got the best of him. 'Everything is all right, Link. I can handle this. Let it go. If I need you I'll call for it, O.K.? Now let's play poker.'

Link slowly turned away from the table, fighting his own instincts to stay. He knew Lola was right, but hated to let someone like Campbell insult him like that and get away with it. It went down hard, but that was part of his job to keep the peace and not make every night a bloody brawl.

Campbell turned back to the table. He'd accomplished what he'd come in for. His men now had a good look at Bonner and couldn't make a mistake in identifying him. He deftly turned up the corner of his cards. A pair of hidden aces winked back at him. A smile lit his pudgy face. Tonight was going to be his night in more ways than one.

CHAPTER EIGHT

Link and Lola sat at the bar, sipping drinks after their shifts were over at four a.m.. It had been an evening of high emotion with J.J. Campbell's sudden appearance, made even stranger by the four men that came in later, standing behind him to make their presence known. Those four worried Lola. They weren't gamblers or just curious onlookers. There was something sinister about them. Now she brought it up with Link.

'Did you notice those four men standing behind J.J. when you came over to my table?'

'I did. What about them?'

'They weren't gamblers. They must have been friends of his and I didn't like their looks either. They were rough and dirty. Why would they even come in here?'

'I don't know, but I wouldn't worry about it. It's been a long night. Why don't we go home and relax? I'll get a big fire going. How's that sound?' He took her hand in his, squeezing it gently as she smiled back, nodding as they got to their feet.

On fall nights like this the brawling, three-hundred mile long Sacramento River sent towering walls of thick, grey fog drifting up its tree-lined banks, spreading its misty fingers out across the valley for miles on end. Even in broad daylight it was impossible to see more than fifty feet in any direction, sometimes lasting all day long. At night everything became mere shadows like drifting ghosts.

Link and Lola stepped outside Ming Too's into that fog-bound world. They walked to the cobblestone curb, trying to look up the street for Sam and his buggy. It was impossible to see whether he was coming down the street or not.

'Hey, Bonner,' a voice called out from twenty feet away up the sidewalk. 'Here's a little message from Mr Campbell for you!'

The sudden flashes and thunder of four pistols shattered the night as Link stabbed for the little Remington in his vest with one hand, pulling Lola down behind him with the other, as bullets tore into them. Link freed the derringer, firing twice in quick succession. Two filmy figures reeled back, crying out in pain, going down, their accomplices firing again before turning to run, swallowed up in fog. Link lay on the ground on his back fumbling for extra cartridges, reloading the pistol by feel. Rolling over, he saw one of the wounded men trying to pull himself up to his feet. Link cocked the hammer, firing both barrels as fast as he could pull the trigger. The shadowed man collapsed again, face down. This time he did not move.

'Lola. . . .' He reached around behind him slowly, rolling painfully over on his side. His hand felt the soft silkiness of her dress, before a dizzying world overtook him. The last thing he heard was the rustle of running feet and the shouts of people coming out of the club, before he lost consciousness and his world went black.

Four days later Link awoke to fuzzy images standing over him, fading in and out. A wall of pain engulfed him the instant he tried to move, causing him to groan out loud.

'Just lay still, Mr Bonner,' a woman's voice ordered. 'If you don't, you'll start bleeding again. Can you understand what I'm saying?'

The face of an older lady with graying hair, slowly swam into view. She was wearing a white cap and dress, and leaned closer, carefully dabbing a damp cloth across Link's sweaty face.

'What . . . happened . . . where am I?' He finally got the words out.

'You're in the Miners' Hospital here in town. We didn't think you were going to pull through for a while. You have three bullet wounds. Doctor Cantrell took one out of your upper chest and the other, your hip. The third grazed the side of your face. That's why we have your head bandaged up like this. You are either very strong or very lucky, Mr Bonner. Most men would not have made it with all the bleeding you've had. Now that you're conscious, I think you've got a real chance to recuperate, but that will take time and pain.'

Link tried to remember all that happened, the ambush gunfight outside of Ming Too's, the image of four men suddenly firing at him as he dug for his vest gun, the two he shot before he and Lola went down wounded.

'Where is . . . Lola? Is she here . . . someplace? Is she . . . all right?' He struggled with the words.

The nurse straightened up, looking at her assistant across the bed. Neither woman spoke. Link tried twisting his head to see who she was staring at. The throbbing head-wound stopped him instantly.

'Answer me . . . where is she?'

'Please listen to me, Mr Bonner. You better concentrate

104

on getting yourself well and not get upset about anything else, at least not now. You're still weak and need all the rest you can get. We'll talk about this. . . .'

'Where is she, damn it!' he cut her off, shivering with frustration.

The woman took in a deep breath, slowly shaking her head before answering. 'Miss Montenegro did not pull through like you did. She passed away the morning both of you were brought in here. She was buried the next day. I'm sorry to have to tell you this, but you insisted. When she knew she was dying, she made me promise to tell you two things. She made me swear to them.'

'What . . . two things?' Tears began to fill Link's eyes, his swollen face twisting in pain, trying not to cry out loud.

'She said she wanted you to have her house . . . and that she loved you deeply.'

He couldn't answer, but choked with emotion, began to cry. His whole world came crashing down around him, including all the plans he and Lola had made for the future. Now there was no future without her. Writhing in misery, vengeance was the only thought he had left.

Bonner stayed at the Miners' Hospital another two weeks before being able to stand and walk haltingly with the aid of a cane. Throughout those days of misery, he kept remembering one thing over and over, the words one of the killers called out an instant before they began firing. 'Here's a little message from Mr Campbell for you!'

It was Campbell who had ordered his killing, and the name burned itself into his mind every waking moment. Nothing else mattered now but finding Campbell and killing him. Link cared naught for his own life, safety or whatever the future might hold. J.J. Campbell would dominate his thoughts day and night. The nights were worst of all.

*

The sun of a cold afternoon, was sinking fast towards the Coast Range Mountains to the west, when a rickety buggy rattled to a stop in front of Lola Montenegro's house. Bonner sat for a moment looking at the adobe-covered home. What he wouldn't give if only Lola could walk out on the front porch one more time, to greet him with one of her loving smiles, he thought.

'We're here, Mr Bonner. I have to get this buggy back to the hospital pretty quick.' The young driver broke into Link's daydream.

'Ah . . . yeah sure, kid. Thanks for the ride.' He grabbed his cane, carefully lowering himself to the ground, heading for the front porch. Step by step he slowly climbed to the top. At the front door he inserted a key into the lock, hesitating a moment. Twisting it, he pushed the door open, stepping inside, leaning on the cane. The room was cold and silent with the musty smell of disuse. He took in a deep breath, steadying himself, walking to the fireplace still stacked with fresh wood he'd left so many weeks ago. Lighting it, he sat on the hearth to the crackle of building flames, looking around the room as shadows danced off the walls and his mind raced with thoughts of Lola and him.

Across the room the bedroom door stood shut. He stared at it a long time before getting back up, then over to the couch. Sitting down he wondered if he should try sleeping in there under its luscious pile of gaudily-colored blankets. If he did, it would be alone, without the feel of Lola's warm, inviting body next to him with his arm wrapped around her as they usually slept. He decided, tonight and for many more nights there after, he'd sleep

106

on the couch, avoiding the bedroom. He was home but in a lifeless house where his only company would be memories. But memories couldn't keep you warm at night or hold you tight. They could only haunt you.

In the days that followed, Link strapped on his six-gun again, enjoying its old, familiar feeling. The little derringer went into a drawer. If only he'd had the big wheel gun that foggy night when he and Lola were ambushed outside of Ming Too's; he was certain everything would have turned out differently. He was convinced Lola would still be alive today. Link began taking the short walk to the American River each day, practicing at getting his hand speed back with the wheel gun. His body was still racked with pain from bullet wounds, and his reflexes were slow. When he grew physically tired he sat on a sandy hummock watching the river flowing by, hurrying to meet the mighty Sacramento River just around the bend. It was peaceful and quiet after all the gunfire, with only the sound of rushing water and gurgling riffles. Slowly, day after day, his draw began to improve. He became faster, more accurate, sending his bullets into a target, the thick trunk of an old cottonwood tree, forty feet away. After another ten days he walked up to inspect the bullet hits. Most of his shots were centered in a fifteen-inch circle, the same width as a man's body, the same as J.J. Campbell's body.

One afternoon, walking back to the house, a lone rider came into view as Link was mounting the front porch stairs. He stopped, studying the unfamiliar figure until the rider came closer, recognizing Mack Bullock, the bartender at Ming Too's. Bullock reined to a stop with a big smile on his face. Getting down, he came up and both men locked hands.

'How are you, Link? Long time no see. It's great to see

you back on your feet again. You have to know everyone at the club was shocked to hear about what happened to you and Lola. She was such a lovely lady, and had so many friends. Folks are still wondering how something like that could take place? She didn't have an enemy in the world, as far as we knew.'

'She was a special lady to me too, Mack. We planned on getting married.' He didn't elaborate further. 'What brings you way out here?'

'Ming sent me. He told me to tell you your job is waiting any time you feel good enough to come back to work. He thought a whole lot of Lola too. He knows how close you two had become. He even sent word out to his oriental friends, trying to find out who ambushed you and her that night. He has a lot of connections on the streets. They found out the two men you shot down worked for J.J. Campbell, at the Embarcadero. They were foremen for work crews that loaded his barges.'

'Campbell.' The name passed Link's lips as a sinister whisper. 'I thought he had to be the one. Now I know I was right. You tell Ming I said thanks for the information, but I'm not ready to go back to work yet. I still have some personal business to take care of. When I'm done with that, I might be able to . . . if I'm still around.'

'I sure will tell him, but you better be careful, Link. Campbell has a lot of friends, and from what I hear they're not all just political ones either. There's a dark side to him most people only whisper about. Know what I mean, Link?'

'I do, but that's the way this is going to play out when I find him. I'm going to make him pay for what he did, and I won't stop until I do. Thanks for coming out here and telling me all this. Thank Ming, too.'

Three days later, Bonner walked down the docks at the Embarcadero, while men loaded barges and the American paddle-wheeler came into sight downstream, announcing its arrival with three long, ear-shattering blasts from its steam-whistle. Link stopped a moment, turning to watch the four-storied vessel come nearer, flags flying, its twin stacks belching clouds of thick, black smoke.

'She's a sight to see, isn't she?' A well-dressed man wearing a top hat, came up alongside Link, as the vessel maneuvered closer.

He turned, eyeing the stranger. 'I imagine so.' He didn't encourage more conversation.

'I couldn't help but notice you're packing that big hog-leg on your hip. Mighty powerful hand-gun, isn't it?'

'It'll do the job if I do mine,' Link answered.

'And from the looks of all that fancy leatherwork on your rig, I'd surmise you're a man who has done his, if you don't mind me saying so.'

Link wondered what the man was driving at with all his talk. His next comment answered that question.

'I hope you'll excuse me for asking, but haven't I seen you before at Ming Too's Red Dragon's Den? I stop in there once in a while for a quick wager.'

'I used to work there.' Link nodded.

'Ah, I thought you looked familiar. You sort of policed the place for Ming, didn't you?'

'I did, but don't remember seeing you there.'

'That's because I didn't make a habit of it. I'm not a regular customer like most other men are. I'm a business man here on the Embarcadero. My trade goods come in from San Francisco on this *American Queen* right here. That's why I'm down here today, to have my men pick them up. I own a trading post a few blocks away in town.'

109

'You happen to know a man named J.J. Campbell?' Link's interest suddenly rose.

'Campbell, sure I do. Everyone down here knows him. He owns most of those barges you see tied up here at the docks. He's my biggest competitor. Is he a friend of yours?'

'A friend? Not likely, but I am looking for him. Do you know if he's around here someplace?'

'I don't believe he is. In fact, I haven't seen him in weeks, and that is unusual. He's generally down here running his foremen, especially when the *American Queen* comes in.'

'Where are these foremen of his?'

'They should be in that shack at the end of the dock. If you walk down there you'll see the sign over the door, 'Campbell Enterprises'. You know, now that you mention him, it seems like someone told me some time back he might have taken the Queen back down to San Francisco. I forgot about that until you brought it up. By the way, my name is Morton Ledbetter. Sorry for such an informal introduction. And yours, sir?' He extended his clean, white hands.

'It's Bonner, Link Bonner.'

'It's been a pleasure meeting you, Mr Bonner. Stop by my store any time you're down town. You may find something you like. I've got a little bit of everything. With all these prospectors coming and going, I've got everything from gold pans to canvas pants plus flour and wheat. I even stock some ammunition for that six-gun of yours.'

Link turned for the shack at the far end of the dock, his mind racing with this new information. If Ledbetter was right, and Campbell had fled to San Francisco, he might have to go there to find him. As he approached the grey, board shack, his hand dropped down feeling the cool, walnut grips on his six-gun. The familiar emotion of a sudden showdown coursed through his body. These might be some of the same men that tried to kill him. At the door Link eased the six-gun out of its holster with his right hand, gripping the doorknob with his left. Twisting it open he slammed his body through the doorway into the dimly lit room, seeing a rough-looking man sitting at a desk, going over paper work. Link's explosive entry caused the man to kick back from the desk, tipping his chair over onto the floor with him still in it. Before he could struggle back to his feet, Link was over the top of him, pointing his wheel gun straight down into the man's face.

'Who . . . the hell . . . are you!' The petrified dock foreman was almost shouting, looking down the gaping, .45 caliber hole in the barrel of Bonner's pistol.

'Where's J.J. Campbell?' Link demanded, pushing the six-gun even closer.

'I don't . . . know no Campbell,' he pleaded, vigorously shaking his head.

'Yes, you do. Open your mouth!'

'What?' His eyes widened as the sweat of fear began popping out on his whiskered face.

'I said open your mouth, or I'll pry it open.'

'My . . . mouth . . . what for?'

Link reached down, grabbing the man by his jacket, pulling him up higher until the barrel of the six-gun pushed hard against his mouth.

'Open up!' he shouted, until the man barely opened, and Link shoved the cold, steel barrel half-way down his throat as he gagged, twisting on the floor.

'I'm going to ask you just one more time. If I don't get a quick answer, I'll blow your head clean off your body, understand?'

111

The victim's eyes widened as he fought for breath until Link slowly withdrew the barrel from his mouth. 'Where is he?'

'He ... and a couple of friends ... went to San Francisco, to hold up a while. That's all I know ... honest.'

'Where at in San Francisco, what friends, give me their names?'

'Maybe they're at the Niantic Hotel. He stays there ... sometimes. It's an old ship beached on high ground.'

'What about the other two? Who are they, and were they in on the shooting in front of Ming Too's last month?'

The foreman slowly nodded, his face and body still rigid with fear. 'It was ... Matt Dern and Billy Sykes did that. I told you ... all I know. For God's sake don't kill me now.'

Link stood up, holstering the six-gun, with one last question, the foreman slowly struggled to his feet, facing him. 'How did those three get to the city?'

'They took the *American Queen*. She's docked here ... now.'

'You keep your mouth shut about this. If you don't, I'll tell everyone on the dock you ratted out your friends, understand? You know what they'll do to you.'

The beaten foreman hung his head, wiping tears and sweat from his face with the back of his shirt sleeve, nodding without answering. Before he looked up again the door slammed, and Link Bonner was gone.

The stiff breeze blowing up the Sacramento River, felt good on Bonner's face, standing at the handrail on the top deck of the *American Queen* trailing billows of black smoke behind it. Brawling, bustling San Francisco lay nearly seventy watery miles away to the west, a three-day trip for the big paddle-wheeler. Link needed that time to come up with a plan to find and kill J.J. Campbell. He envisioned the showdown over and over. Would Campbell get down on his hands and knees, pleading for his life, whimpering like a child, or would he promise money or anything else he wanted just to let him live. Would he still have Matt Dern and Billy Sykes protecting him? If he did, he'd have to take down all three of them at the same time, even though he'd never seen either man before. That wouldn't be a problem. They'd have to be sticking close to their boss. Neither of them could match his hand-speed and Campbell, even if he was armed, had likely never pulled a gun on anyone in his entire life. A man like that freezes in fear when six-guns are being pulled. All Link had to do was find them. The sooner the better.

Late on the afternoon of the third day, Bonner came out on deck bundled in warm clothes, heavy coat, wide-brimmed hat and a silk neck-scarf Lola had given him as a gift. The American Queen was churning across open bay waters with dirty whitecaps lapping at her sides. A throng of people stood at the rail, pointing and gesturing across the water as a massive, slow-motion fog bank crept through hills in from the ocean, beginning to obscure an endless line of tall sailing ships anchored against the shoreline, their masts empty of sails and decks devoid of men. Beyond the ships the outline of many buildings marked waterfront businesses the fast-growing city was so famous for. Backing them, rolling hills with scattered houses were beginning to disappear as the advancing wall of fog climbed grassy slopes in its misty embrace.

'Look at all those ships.' One woman at the rail pointed with a gloved hand. 'I don't think you could get another one in there, they're so close together.'

'It said in the paper that most of them are abandoned. Their captains and crews dropped anchor and left them high and dry, all heading for the goldfields up in the Sierra Nevadas,' her companion answered.

Link studied the buildings along the shoreline, vanishing in fog. J.J. Campbell had to be in one of them as well as his two assassins, thinking they were safe from any ramifications of Lola's killing, left behind in Sacramento. Link remembered what the foreman at the Embarcadero had said. Campbell might be at the Niantic Hotel. He'd try there first, soon as the *American Queen* docked.

Scurrying men wrapped thick, woven hawsers around mooring posts, securing the big paddle-wheeler to the dock. The gangplank was lowered as a crowd of passengers carrying suitcases and duffle bags, slowly exited the ship while Bonner stood watching them go. When the gangplank emptied he adjusted the six-gun on his hip, the last one off the *American Queen*. A short walk brought him to Montgomery Street, engulfed in a throng of men moving on both sides. It seemed the entire planet had suddenly descended on the city, swelling it to overflowing. Men on horses rode down the busy street along with mule-drawn carts, followed by barking dogs. Chinese, Mexicans, Germans, Spaniards and Irishmen along with some blacks made up the jostling crowd, each speaking in their own strange tongue, wearing odd traditional clothes and hats. Link had never seen such a mix of people before, not even in Sacramento. Coal-oil lamps burning in saloons, gambling houses, dry goods and feed stores plus several boat-works, lit both sides of the street in a mellow glow.

Link stepped back out of the crowd, leaning on a building for a moment, taking it all in, wondering what his chances were to find Campbell in this endless amalgam of humanity. A short, red-headed man wearing a checkered cap came by, speaking rapidly to two friends in a thick, Irish brogue. Link hailed him with a question.

'Do any of you men know where the Niantic Hotel is?'

The Irishman cocked his head, eyeing Bonner up and down before answering.

'For sure we do, me man. New in town, huh? Who isn't?' He laughed. 'You stay on this walker another block. It's right near the corner just down from the Eagle Saloon, a favorite place of me and me pals here.'

'Thanks.' Link nodded, pushing back into the bustling crowd. Half a block later, he felt a hand trying to slip into his jacket pocket. Before the thief could extract anything, Link grabbed the pick-pocket's arm, twisting it so violently the man fell to the ground screaming, his arm broken. Link dropped on top of him, pinning his shoulders to the ground, sending a crashing right hand to his jaw, knocking the scrawny little man unconscious. The moving crowd parted only briefly, eyeing the confrontation then closed ranks before moving on while some laughed out loud at the failed attempt.

'Dat Scaly, got his self caught again.' A large black man wearing a frayed straw hat and bib overalls, stopped a moment, shaking his head and looking down. 'One of des days someone gonna put a knife in his sneaky fingers.'

'Or a bullet in him,' Bonner answered. 'You know him?'

'Sure do. He always picken' pockets of people new in

town. Usually makes good money too, if he don't get caught. But not wit' you. You too fast for 'em.'

Link got to his feet as the big man turned back into the crowd and disappeared, everyone seemingly unconcerned about what had just happened. So, this was San Francisco, Link thought. Life must be cheap here. If that's the way they wanted it, he'd give them two or three more men to ignore, and with pleasure.

Further along Montgomery Street, Bonner came to a stop across from the Niantic Hotel. The odd sight of the ship's bow sitting on dry ground, sticking out into the street didn't seem to faze those passing. Where masts had once been, a two-story hotel was built atop the old deck. A set of steps led up on the right side to the front door. Another smaller, beached vessel now used as a warehouse, sat next to the Eagle Saloon two doors down. If the foreman back in Sacramento was telling the truth, finally facing and killing J.J. Campbell could be only seconds away. Link took in a deep breath. He'd sworn to avenge Lola's death at any cost. Now he'd honor that vow. He started across the busy street, pushing his way through people, toward the hotel.

Inside the Niantic he stood a moment taking in the strange scene. The misty smell of salt air and sea still permeated the entire hull from all those years plying the Pacific Ocean, hunting whales. A small counter table held a register, but no one to man it. Link stepped up to the counter, opening the book, searching the names of occupants. On the second page scrawled in black ink, the name J.J. Campbell stood out in large scroll. Directly below the signature were the names of Dern and Sykes. None of the trio listed Sacramento as their home. The sound of faltering footsteps was followed by a bald-headed old man coming out of a back room where he'd obviously been

117

napping. His wrinkled clothes and half-buttoned shirt were soiled with age.

'We're full up. We aint't got no room to rent,' the old-timer snapped. 'You'll have to try someplace else, good night.' He started turning around.

'Wait a minute. Your register here says a man named J.J. Campbell and two friends are staying here. Are they still?'

'I don't keep no tabs on anyone. Ain't got time for it so long as they pay their bill. If they don't, I throw them out right quick.' He reached under the counter, retrieving a stout, hardwood club, shaking it at Bonner.

'So, you don't know if Campbell is still here or not? Is that what you're saying?' Link challenged.

'Are your ears plugged? I said I don't keep no tabs on anyone. Besides, if he was, Mr Campbell would likely be a couple of doors down at the Eagle Saloon, or maybe over at the bull ring visiting the "ladies". Just remember I don't know if none of it's true, and you forget where you ever heard it, you understand, Mr?'

'Yeah, I understand. Thanks for not keeping tabs on your guests.' Link pushed a silver dollar across the counter to the old man, exiting the Niantic with a grim smile on his lips.

Three doors down from the hotel, the wooden two-story building of the Eagle Saloon stood out, its name boldly emblazoned across the second-floor front. Men steadily pushed in and out of the front door of the popular drinking establishment. Link's hand went down for the familiar feel of walnut grips on his six-gun. If Campbell was in there, he'd kill him straight away without a call. If his two pals were with him, he'd take them down just as quick. Stepping inside he edged up against the wall, eyes searching the noisy, smoke-filled room. Drinkers crowded the bar. Gambling tables were filled, every seat taken, as curious onlookers stood behind players, watching money change hands. Not seeing Campbell, Bonner began circulating around the room, going from table to table to be certain he wasn't there. Frustrated at his failure, he pushed his way over to the bar where a big man with a curly, handlebar mustache was pouring drinks.

'You know a man named J.J. Campbell?' he asked the counter-man over the loud talk of others around him.

'Do I look like a walking dictionary?' the bar-man shot back sarcastically.

'I didn't ask for the shirt off your back,' Bonner fired back.

'And you're not drinking either. You want everything for free, huh?'

Bonner reached into his vest pocket, pushing a gold half-eagle across the counter. 'I'll have a whiskey. Does that help?'

The big man reached under the counter, bringing up a bottle and stubby glass, filling it to the brim with amber-colored liquid. 'Now what was that name again?'

'Campbell, J.J. Campbell. He might be traveling with two friends.'

'Oh, yeah, I think I know him, and no he hasn't been in here tonight. At least not yet. It's still early. I did hear he lost a bundle last night at the poker table.'

'I'm new in town. Are there any other popular gambling spots around here?'

'Any other? San Francisco is full of them. They're the life blood that keep this town running day and night. There's the Exchange, the Veranda, Aquila de Oro, the Bella Union, to name just a few big ones. If I were you I'd try the Bella. It does the most business for big spenders

119

like Campbell. It's three blocks up the street.'

'Thanks.' Bonner downed the shot in one quick hook, heading for the front door.

The Bella Union catered to the city's high rollers, rich and affluent men in business and politics who could bet thousands of dollars on just one turn of the card or a one-second stroke of luck. Major games in the Bella were Mexican Monte, faro, poker and roulette. Fortunes were won and lost at its tables, and those that did not have the money to play, always showed up just to watch the fascinating action. Link stepped through the front door, immediately confronted by two large men dressed in expensive suits, blocking further entry. Their scarred, emotionless faces and thick beards belied the fancy clothes.

'You can't come in here with that hog-leg on your hip,' one man said. 'This is a gentleman's club, not some saloon-slop crowd down on the waterfront. Give up the gun or turn around and leave.'

Link hesitated, sizing up the pair. He couldn't shoot his way in without causing a riot. He had to walk in on Campbell, if he was here, surprising him and anyone with him instead of putting him on the run again. Link looked from man to man before slowly unbuckling his gun-belt, handing the rig over.

'You get it back when you leave. Now you can enter,' one of the guards said.

When Bonner walked into the room, one look was all it took to make it clear the Bella was a much different establishment than the Eagle or just about anyplace else. The usual noise and shouting of excited men at gambling tables was gone. In its place, most men wore fine clothes and expensive hats, while a trio of ladies adorned in fancy dresses with stylish hairdos, circulated from table to table, serving drinks, lighting cigars, or making cash deliveries from the bank cage to players needing more money.

Bonner slowly walked past roulette wheels and faro games, eyeing each player as he went. None was Campbell. Along the far wall a line of poker games also drew large crowds of both players and watchers, making it impossible to see who was sitting at the tables. Stepping into the crowd at the first table, he looked from man to man. Still no sign of Campbell. Backing out he approached the next table in line. The dealer, an attractive Asian woman with black hair tied in a bun, and ruby-red lips, looked up momentarily at him before going back to her cards. Seeing a woman dealer so unexpectedly, sent a shock of grief through Link, remembering his beloved Lola, the same grief that had driven him all the way here to San Francisco.

From where he was standing, Link could see the next poker table and its players. Instantly he recognized one man with his back to him, hat off, his thinning, light-brown hair and fat neck protruding above the collar. It was J.J. Campbell at last! He sat hunched over, studying another losing hand, trying to bluff his way into winning a large pile of money in the middle of the table. Link fought to control the rage coursing through him by studying the two men standing directly behind Campbell. They looked out of place, their faces unshaven, clothes rumpled. The pair had to be Matt Dern and Billy Sykes, Campbell's two body guards. Bonner pulled his hat lower over his face, quietly backing out of the knot of men. He couldn't kill Campbell right here in this crowded room. Innocent bystanders would surely catch bullets if he tried. He quickly decided now that he'd found Campbell and

121

identified his pals, he'd take them outside when they exited the Bella.

Bonner retrieved his six-gun at the check-in counter before stepping back outside into the growing dark of early evening. Already, thickening fog off San Francisco Bay began to further shroud the street in wet, grey mist. Passers by loomed up out of the obscure wall only to disappear back into it seconds later. Link could not help but remember it was on a foggy night back in Sacramento when he and Lola were ambushed, and she was killed. Was it black fate that made this showdown unfold under exactly the same circumstances, or just a lucky spin of the roulette wheels inside the Bella Union. Either way, Link had vowed to empty a six-gun into J.J. Campbell and kill his two shooters if they tried to stop him. He wanted Campbell to go down on the ground, writhing in pain with a belly full of hot lead.

The endless stream of gamblers going in and out of the Bella caused a sudden flash of light illuminating the street every time the front door was opened. Bonner stationed himself in shadows against the wall just back from the door so he would not be highlighted. Every time someone exited the building, he took a few steps forward, six-gun in his hand ready to call out Campbell. After more than an hour later squaring off against strangers, he began to think Campbell was either going to spend the entire night gambling, or had left by another exit. The fog grew even thicker, its cold, clammy fingers encasing the city in its grip. Bonner pulled his jacket collar higher, massaging his hands to keep circulation going. Men continued to enter and exit the building, but none were Campbell.

Link's patience was nearly gone when he decided to go back inside to see if Campbell was still there. He'd just started for the door when it opened and Campbell, along with Dern and Sykes, one on either side of him, walked out. Link quickly pulled his jacket open clearing his six-gun with a shout.

'Campbell, it's time you paid up for killing Lola!' His voice cut through the night like a razor, freezing the three men in their tracks.

For just an instant Campbell wasn't sure who had shouted the sudden demand but knew it was not Billy Sykes or Matt Dern. Sykes was on his boss' left side nearest Bonner. Instantly he went for his six-gun, both he and Link firing fast shots at the same time. Sykes' pistol clattered to the street and he began sinking to his knees, grabbing his chest. Campbell screamed at the roar of sudden shots, ducking around Dern, running into the dark. Dern jerked his revolver from its holster while jumping back into the entrance alcove, out of sight for a moment. Link ran out into the street where he could see Dern up against the wall. Both men fired in rapid succession until Dern slowly slid down the wall into a sitting position, eyes open, his pistol still in the hands of a dead man.

Campbell, where did he go? Link turned in a fast circle as the front door burst open and the two guards pushed outside, pistols in their hands. Before they could react, Link sprinted away into the dark the same direction he'd last seen Campbell flee.

The streets were wet and slippery, dimly lit by light from all night businesses. Bonner ran block after block searching for a glimpse of Campbell someplace ahead. His breath came in short gasps as he ran on until he became aware of something warm and wet soaking through his shirt. He was hit, but wasn't sure how bad or even where.

123

The growing pain in his hip didn't matter. He had to stay on his feet and keep running. Somewhere in the foggy night ahead, Campbell was running too, running for his very life. Link couldn't let him get away now, not after all he'd done to find him.

Barely a block ahead, Campbell was on his last legs. He slipped and went down, rolling on the street, struggling to pull himself back up and run on. He knew who he was running from now. There was no mistaking Link Bonner's voice back at the Bella Union. Campbell's wobbly legs were giving out on him. His lungs ached for a full breath, if he could only stop running, but he could not. Suddenly, in the foggy dark, he could smell the distinct odor of bay water. Shadowed buildings fell away behind him as he stumbled onto a narrow pier jutting out into the bay, the sound of his boots on wooden planks echoing. He groped his way forward. Maybe he could find a row boat to flee in, or something even larger to hide in. He stopped, head down, hands on his knees, gasping for air, trying to suck in a full breath. He couldn't run another yard. He was played out.

When he finally straightened up he became aware of new dark shadows looming around him. What were they? He looked closer, finally able to make out the black hulls of abandoned sailing ships, their empty masts reaching up into the night like so many bony fingers, as they rose and fell to the watery slap of swells. Cold sweat poured down Campbell's chubby face. He pulled a fancy, embroidered handkerchief from his jacket with the initials 'J.J.C.', mopping his face. That's when he heard another sound behind him in the dark, the sound of boots coming steadily closer on the wooden planks. J.J. tried to run, stumbling farther down the pier, sheer panic wracking his body. Suddenly he pulled up short. The pier ended in foggy nothingness. There was no place left to run. He was trapped. He reached out, grabbing the last, slimy piling to steady himself, staring wide-eyed back into the fog as those boot steps came closer. His mind raced for some way out. There had to be a way to save himself.

A misty shadow materialized out of the fog, coming to a stop just yards away. Campbell choked, trying to get the words out, begging not to be killed. He held up both hands, pleading for mercy he'd never shown anyone else.

'I . . . didn't know Lola was with you . . . that night. You gotta believe me . . . I'll pay you . . . I've got money. I'll give you . . . anything you want. A thousand dollars . . . five-thousand . . . even ten. Just don't . . . pull that trigger!'

'You're the kind of slimy scum that drives people to murder. You've driven me to it right here and now. You took the only thing I ever loved and killed her. Now you're going to get what you've got coming to you, and no amount of money can buy your way out of it. I've taken care of your friends. You're all that's left.'

'No, look here.' Campbell pulled out his wallet removing a thick sheaf of bills, thrusting them out to Bonner. 'They're all yours. Go ahead and take it. There's lots more back in Sacramento too. All you have to do is let me live and you can have all of it. That's all I'm asking. . . .'

The thunder of a single pistol shot and spear of flame from Link's six-gun echoed into the foggy night across the unseen bay. The bullet impact sent J.J. Campbell reeling backwards off the dock, sinking into icy water, as paper money fluttered down around him like autumn leaves. Link holstered the revolver, standing a moment longer knowing he'd just turned into a cold-blooded murderer himself. All the other showdowns and gunfights were done

CHAPTER TEN

In front of the Bella Union, a crowd of men gathered on the street, talking excitedly, watching the bodies of Matt Dern and Billy Sykes loaded onto a wagon. They shouted questions back and forth amongst each other and the door guards.

'This is murder, pure and simple!' one man's voice rose above the others.

'Yeah, we all know San Francisco is still a little rough around the edges, but gunning down people right out on the street is just too much. Hell, it could be any of us gets the same thing!' another seconded, to the crowd's noisy approval.

From out of the Bella strode a neatly-dressed man with a well-trimmed mustache and wearing a bowler hat, eyeing boisterous onlookers a moment before he stepped up and turned his attention to the guards. His name was Rebus Thornberry, head of the city's Committee of Vigilantes, a citizen's organization that administered its own brand of justice called 'rope law', in the absence of any real formal police department.

Thornberry surveyed the pair of dead men laid out in the cart, before posing a question to the two men.

'Did you get a good look at the men who did this?' he questioned.

'It wasn't men,' one guard answered. 'It was only one man. We disarmed him earlier this evening when he came into the club.'

'One man took down these two? He must be some kind of mad-dog killer to do something like that. You both got a good look at him?'

'We did. We don't have a name, but I'd know him anywhere by the way he was dressed.'

'Like what?'

'He wore a wide-brimmed cowboy hat, dark jacket and pants with high-heeled riding boots. He also had a six-gun on his hip with a fancy leather rig full of cartridges. He wasn't one of the usual crowd, you know sailors, prospectors, gamblers or business men. He looked like he belonged in some cow town on a horse, not in the Bella Union.'

'He ran down the street that way towards the docks,' the other guard pointed.

'I'm going to deputize you both right now,' Thornberry announced. 'We're going after him and I'll take some of these other men with us too. Let's get our hands on him before he gets too far away, or kills anyone else. I'll make an example out of him no one in this town will ever forget. Dancing a jig at the end of a rope will make an impression on others like him. I can guarantee you that. Now raise your right hands.'

Bonner stepped off the dock, back onto the street, stopping a moment to refill the empty chamber of his pistol. No sooner had he done so when he heard noisy voices up the street, coming closer even though no one was in sight yet. Quickly crossing the street, he stepped into the shadows of a narrow alley between two buildings. When a crowd of men carrying flaming torches came into view, he recognized the guards from the Bella Union, but not a smaller man between them who seemed to be leading everyone, and carried a coiled rope over his shoulder. Stopping at the pier, he began shouting orders.

'The guards and I will take the pier. You men split up into two groups. One of you head down the shoreline to the west. The rest of you search back along the dock warehouses to the east, and be careful. We've already had two killings tonight. I don't want any more. Now, let's get to it!'

When flickering torch lights disappeared into the night, Link stepped out of the alley, pausing a moment to be certain he was alone. It was clear he had to get out of San Francisco fast and away from the vigilantes hunting him. The only option was the way he'd come, the *American Queen*. Was the big vessel still tied up at the wharf? He had to find out quickly.

Thornberry and the guards carefully made their way out along the pier, pistols drawn, a torch in one man's hand. Silent shadows of sailing ships rose out of fog on each side and passed as they went. Fifteen minutes later the three men reached the end of the pier. Thornberry took the torch from one of the men, edging out on the last plank, holding the flaming club high over his head, eyes searching out into the swirling wall of grey. Only the watery gurgle of moving water met his ears. One of the men stepped up alongside him, slipping his revolver back into his jacket holster.

'He sure as hell ain't out there,' he commented, before something caught his eye on the reflected water right below them. 'What's that?' He directed Thornberry's attention straight down.

Revel lowered the torch, stooping down, the ghastly image of J.J. Campbell's body floating face up, staring back at them with dead eyes.

'Good God, it's Campbell,' he gasped. 'Quick, we've got to fish him out of the water!'

'What's that other stuff around him?' the second man said.

Thornberry pushed the torch even lower. 'Why, it's . . . paper money . . . lots of it. That killer must have chased him all the way out here. When the poor devil couldn't run any further, he shot him down in cold blood. If the Committee has to turn this town upside down to find this murderer, we will. An animal like that has to be exterminated just like any rabid dog!'

Bonner moved through the night, down empty streets, avoiding the lights and nightlife of the city. He didn't dare go back near the Bella Union, and the familiar short walk from the wharf where the *American Queen* had tied up. Instead he got lost in a maze of narrow, unlit streets and alleys shrouded in thick fog. Hours later he finally found his way back to the waterfront where the big paddle-wheeler was tied up. Edging closer he saw four armed men forming a line across the gangplank leading onto the tall vessel. The vigilantes had already posted them here to stop his escape. Link eased back into the dark, his mind working on how to get past them onto the big boat.

Now that he'd stopped running, the bullet wound on his hip began burning like fire again. He loosened his belt, running his hand down to the bloody handkerchief he'd stuffed into his pants to stem the flow of blood. It was soaked sticky red. Wringing it out he double-folded it, carefully repositioning it, tightening the belt again. A precious hour dragged by that he could not afford to waste, without seeing any way to board the vessel. He could not take on four men in a straight-up gunfight and win. The odds were too great for that. He had to find some other way, but what?

The long dead of night slowly began turning to the first misty grey of dawn, the outline of the big boat growing clearer as each minute passed. Down the street leading to the wharf, the first horse-drawn carts loaded with supplies for Sacramento began to show up, forming a long line waiting to be unloaded. At the gangplank, each load was inspected before being allowed to pass. On heavier loads a long pole-boom was swung out with a cargo net lowered on the end, operated by a man working steam levers to do the lifting. The line of carts and wagons grew even longer as loading slowed until it backed all the way up the street as the morning continued to brighten and the fog began its slow retreat.

Bonner studied the formation of wagons. Just maybe they could be the answer he'd struggled to find on how to board the *American Queen*. If he could somehow work his way into one of those wagons, he might get past the guards without a killing gunfight. The sound of riders on horses coming down the street got his attention. He turned to see Revel Thornberry in the saddle, along with the two guards from the Bella Union, and two other men. Link sank farther back into shadows, watching as Thornberry got down, engaging the men at the gangplank in animated conversation. After a few minutes the original guards shook hands with the new arrivals before starting up the street, leaving their post as Thornberry and his men took over. Link's chances of getting on board seemed to sink even further. Thornberry didn't know him on sight, but the Bella guards did. If he was going to make his move it

131

had to be now. Time was running out.

The pace of loading picked up as more supplies were stacked on the front deck, and the long, waiting line shortened. The dim, silver disk of a rising sun behind thinning blankets of fog began to further light the land, water and wagons. Soon it would burn off into a bright, sunny morning. Link turned away from his hiding place, moving swiftly up the line of shore shanties out of sight until turning back toward the street where the remaining wagons waited to be unloaded. He chose the very last one to step in behind, staying out of view, moving with it as it edged closer to the loading spot. Its heavy load of wooden boxes meant the boatmen would have to use the big cargo net to swing its supplies on board. The line continued to shorten until Link's wagon was finally at the loading spot just as the big steam-whistle on the *Queen* sent out three long blasts announcing steam was up and the vessel was ready to pull out.

The pole boom was swung out and the net lowered while the wagon driver and his two helpers began muscling heavy crates into the net. Link crouched behind the wagon, waiting for the very last moment before making his move. The final boxes were loaded and the wagon driver raised his hand signaling they were done. The boom arm lifted and the rope tightened as the loaded net began rising. Link leaped from behind the wagon onto the bed then vaulted into the net, digging his feet into the webbing while hanging on with one hand, as the load lifted higher and the boatman began reeling in the heavy load.

Those first few seconds Thornberry and his men didn't see Bonner clinging to the back side of the load. Their attention was on the last wagon turning around to start up the empty street. As the net began turning, one of the guards looked up to see Link hanging on with a pistol in his free hand.

'There he is, there's the killer!' he pointed up, shouting at the top of his lungs, drawing his revolver, trying to take aim at the swinging load and its surprising passenger. Revel and the other men twisted their heads, looking up in wide-eyed astonishment, grabbing for their pistols too, the guard firing first once, twice. Link, pulling himself closer to the net, fired back. The guard yelled out in pain, dropping his pistol which clattered off the gangplank into the water, sinking to his knees, grabbing at his stomach. The instant the net crossed the deck, Link dropped onto the floor behind a pile of wooden boxes, firing more shots at the gangplank men without cover. Thornberry twisted to a bullet hit, grabbing at his side, the other men retreating at a crouch onto muddy ground, firing back wildly, running for cover.

Up in the wheelhouse, Captain William Bledsoe, couldn't believe his eyes at the savage gunfight going on below. He didn't know who was who, only that the odds were stacked against the one man boldly taking on four others.

'Raise the gangplank!' he shouted through the talk tube leading to the deck. 'Get it up right now!' He finished as the big wooden paddle-wheels on the *American Queen* began churning choppy water and the vessel slowly inched back away from the landing.

Link quickly reloaded as the unwounded Bella guard rushed forward at a crouch, firing his pistol, wading out into knee-deep water, trying to reach the deck. Link stood up to get a clearer shot, his first bullet kicking up a geyser of spray right in front of the big man. His second and third shots found their mark, the guard grabbing his chest, falling face down into the icy bay water, slowly floating back toward the landing.

Bonner raced up the steps to the top deck, bursting into the wheelhouse, leveling his six-gun on white-bearded Captain Bledsoe who stared back, still in disbelief of what he'd just seen.

'You keep this boat going back at full speed, or I will. You understand me?'

'I do. You can put that revolver down now,' Bledsoe tried to answer calmly as possible. 'No one is going to get on board. We're already out in deep water. Do you want to tell me what all this is about? I've never had a killing on this vessel before. I'd at least like to know why, and so will others I work for once we reach Sacramento.'

Bonner took in a deep breath, trying to decide whether to holster the six-gun or not. 'It's about payback,' he said, lowering the hog-leg but keeping it in his hand. 'I had a score to settle. Now it's done. We're even. That's all you have to know.'

'All right. For now, that will have to do. I'm not a lawman. I'm a ship's captain, and I'm unarmed. I'd like you to put that pistol away before anything else happens. I don't want to see any more people ending up as fish bait.'

Link retreated a few steps to a small seat next to one of the windows. Sitting, he laid the six-gun next to him, the burning pain in his hip returning with renewed vengeance. He leaned back a moment closing his eyes from the sudden fury of the gun battle. The vigilantes were no longer a problem, but he'd never be able to return to San Francisco again. His name and face would be plastered all over town on wanted posters with a huge reward for his capture. The boat trip inland to Sacramento would take three days. He'd worry about what to do next when he got there. Now he needed rest, clean bandages and time to think things through.

Bonner spent most of the three day trip in the wheelhouse, forcing Captain Bledsoe to stay there too. He had Bledsoe order up their meals and bandages. During the night when the captain had to sleep, his replacement at the big wheel guided the vessel further inland with one eye out the front window, the other on Bonner catching a few minutes of sleep only to wake with a start, threatening the terrified stand-in not to try anything. During the day Link would step outside onto the open deck, closing his eyes trying to catch a few more moments of rest. He'd avenged Lola's death, but it was more than likely the murders of J.J. Campbell and his two henchmen would follow him all the way to Sacramento. The vigilantes might even send men after him for what he'd done to them in their town, forcing him back for a trial that could only end in a public hanging. Revel Thornberry wasn't going to forget the crippling wound that would leave him to walk with the aid of a cane the rest of his life, and the loss of his men in the savage dock gunfight. Link realized he might be clear of trouble in the growing city by the bay, but Sacramento could soon become just as dangerous for him when word got out about the killings.

On the morning of the third day, Bonner walked out onto the deck, looking beyond waving lines of tulles and trees lining the entrance to the Sacramento River. Blue in the distance, the irregular outline of the Sierra foothills marched across the horizon and its fabled veins of gold-bearing ore that had lured tens of thousands of men from around the world to strike it rich. Farther back and higher up, jagged peaks capped in snow announced the granite-laced spires of the mighty Sierra Nevada range. As he studied that high country, one thought quickly came to him. Up there he'd be on his own again in the saddle, free of any law and all the threats that went with it. The big country had always been his one true refuge. It was time to ride back into it, leaving everything else behind, the farther away the better.

Late that afternoon the *American Queen*'s big paddle-wheels began to slow as its steam-whistle sent out three long, shrill blasts, approaching its mooring site at the Embarcadero. Bonner stood in the wheelhouse, staring out the window as the vessel edged slowly closer to the wharf until lines were thrown, the ship coming to a stop. He scanned the dock below to be certain no one that looked like the law was waiting for him. Workers lowered the gangplank and began unloading the cargo, stacking it in neat rows on the dock. Captain Bledsoe gave the command to shut down the engine before stepping away from the wheel, studying Bonner a moment before speaking.

'Well, we are back home, and you've not been molested in any way, as I promised. Are you now ready to holster that pistol of yours? It certainly saw enough use in San Francisco to last a while, didn't it?'

Link turned to the white-bearded officer. 'You were smart not to have any of your men try something stupid. All I wanted was a boat ride back here. Now I'll leave, and I would suggest you don't try to raise any alarm when I do.'

'I have no intention of doing that, but I will have to report about all this in the ship's log for the men I work for. Of course, that must include the gun fight on the dock. By the time they read it, I assume you'll be long gone from Sacramento. Now that we're parting company, it strikes me that I never asked your name. Do you mind

136

telling me what it is?'

'It's Bonner, Link Bonner. It won't stay a secret very long, and if anyone asks why I did what I did, you can tell them it was the only way I could get even for what was done to someone I loved deeply, who was murdered by the same people. Now I've settled it for her and myself. You stay up here until you see me walk out of sight off the dock.'

'I said I wouldn't call for help, and I stand by my word. But you do understand the law has to know about all this too, don't you?'

'Yes, I do. I have only two things to do before I ride out of this town. Neither one will take long. The law here will never see me again. Good bye, Captain.'

Bledsoe came to the window, watching his strange passenger with nerves of steel and a fast gun, reach the bottom deck, walking down the gangplank off the boat. A few seconds more he was lost in a crowd of arriving men and horse-drawn wagons eager to begin loading the new supplies. Bledsoe pulled at his well-trimmed beard, talking quietly to himself. 'About as strange a man as I've ever met,' he mused. 'I have to wonder how much longer he thinks his extraordinary luck can hold out?'

Link walked as fast as the pain in his hip would allow, leaving the busy Embarcadero behind. The stable where he'd left his horse lay on the outskirts of town some distance away. He had to get there quickly, pay boarding fees, and do one more important thing he'd promised himself before leaving Sacramento. The afternoon sun was sinking fast toward the Coast Range Mountains, when he turned a corner to the shout of someone behind him. Link spun, drawing his six-gun, hammer cocked, eyes wide for trouble.

137

'Link Bonner, it's me, Samuel Monty, Miss Lola's carriage man!' The driver waved, urging horse and carriage closer up the street. 'I thought that was you but I couldn't tell for sure from behind until you turned around. Put that six-gun away. I don't mean no harm. You remember me, don't you? If you'd like a ride someplace I'd be glad to take you.'

Bonner straightened up, holstering the pistol, letting out a long breath of relief. 'I'm sorry, Sam. I didn't know it was you. It's kind of a habit of mine to pull first and ask later. I'm heading out to Jolly's Stables. If you'd like to give me a ride, I can use it.'

'Sure will, Mr Bonner. This is the first time I've seen you since that terrible night Miss Lola got shot. I sure did love that pretty lady. I don't know who could do a horrible thing like that so someone so nice, do you?'

'Yeah, I do. And I've taken care of it for Lola and myself. Give me a hand getting up, will you?'

'Some people in town said it was a hold up for money, and some say it was an ambush to kill you, that went bad?' Sam stared back, hoping for an answer.

'People can say anything they want. It's over and done with. I really don't want to talk about it any more, Sam. Let's just get out to the stables.'

'I understand, Mr Bonner. I'm sorry I even brought it up, but it's still the talk of the whole town. I know you and Miss Lola were real close, anyone could see that.'

Link couldn't answer this time. The sudden lump in his throat stopped him. All he could do was sit there and choke down a deep breath, while Sam tapped his whip across the horse's back and wheels spun faster down the bumpy street.

The carriage jolted to a stop in front of Jolly's. Link

took in a deep breath, opening it, walking inside. At a chest of drawers next to the big bed, he opened the top one, taking out one of Lola's favorite, bright-red silk scarves. Her fragrance was unmistakable. He carefully folded it, putting inside his vest pocket. It was all of Lola Montenegro he would ever have left to remember her by.

Atop the dresser sat a large, clay coin bank made in the form of a Mexican burro, painted in bright yellows, browns and blacks. He and Lola always put their tip money from Ming's in there and any extra cash for the day they planned to leave Sacramento and start a new life together someplace else. Link stared at the floppy-eared burro, his mind racing with emotion, before picking it up, smashing it down, shattering it. He picked up the coins and paper money, putting it in a leather pouch found in the second drawer. Exiting the room, he walked back to the front door. Lamp in hand, he took one more long, last look around, remembering what might have been, in the only real home he'd ever known since he was a young boy living with his widowed mother. In a fury of savage emotion, he threw the lamp across the floor, instantly igniting the room in a brilliant ball of flame. In seconds it climbed the walls, engulfing the entire room in a roaring inferno.

Bonner backed down the stairs, transfixed at the sight until reaching his horse. Up in the saddle, the skittish animal jerked and danced, whinnying in fear, while Link watched new flames shoot out front windows and the door, the entire structure now a roaring blaze with a shrieking voice of its own. All he and Lola had, all they'd planned together for their future, rose in twisting pillars of flame sending billows of black smoke blotting out a starry sky. It made little difference now what the future held for him back out on his own again. He remembered talk from

Ming's, that far away Denver held another famous gambling house, the Keystone, catering to rich and famous clients. He had no place left to go, and no one who cared where he ended up. Maybe the long ride from Sacramento, Lola and memories of what might have been, could be blurred in Denver. He'd lost everything of value in the bustling gold-rush town by two rivers, wishing to God he'd never come here at all.

CHAPTER ELEVEN

The bitter, month-long ride to Denver through increasing snow flurries and dropping temperatures made arriving a relief. Link easily found the Keystone on a busy street, its name in large letters boldly painted in black across the big, two-story building. Sixty-six-year-old Kurt Keystone, the man who'd brought the famous gambling house to life, ran business affairs from his second-floor office. His daughter, thirty-year-old Katie, ran the first-floor gambling hall tables, bar and private rooms in back for those who didn't wish to be seen gambling. She could be instantly spotted, even on a busy night, by her flaming-red hair in curls down to her shoulders, adorned in expensive gowns from back east. Katie inherited her strong business sense from her white-haired father, making it clear her word was law to both employees and gamblers. No one was going to argue about it either.

Men of wealth and position tried to date her, but Katie always kept her business face and manners as a barrier to avoid personal entanglements. Behind her back, most men concluded she'd never marry anyone, regardless of her engaging conversation and quick smile. She was an iron maiden who seemed only to live to keep the Keystone legacy in tact. When she interviewed Link for the job of floor security, she found him to be slightly older than her, with solid experience from his days in Sacramento, and with a certain maturity that told her he meant what he said and was cock sure of himself. She also noticed he showed not the slightest hint of emotion as they talked through the interview. After Link left, she talked to her father about him, saying she thought they should give him a go on a trial basis to see how he worked out. Kurt agreed but said to keep an eye on him.

In the week that followed, Bonner settled into his new job, quickly becoming known and respected by the Keystone gambling crowd. The ladies especially paid attention to the good-looking new man with coal-black hair and piercing blue eyes. Several often pretended to need his help for some trivial complaint, just to have him come over, engaging in flirtatious conversation. Katie couldn't help but notice the attention he was getting. For some strange reason it began to annoy her. She wasn't sure exactly why. Her association with Link had never become personal. She would not let it, and for his part, Link made no move in showing any more than a business interest in her, keeping things on a professional basis. He'd vowed not to let heartbreak like Lola Montenegro, happen ever again.

One night, just before Link's shift came to an end, Katie decided to try and get some answers to the questions she had about him. She had no other option but to try a direct approach, awkward and uncomfortable as it was for her. The Keystone was emptying out with only a handful of gamblers still at the tables. Even the pair of big roulette wheels had stopped spinning. Link was standing by one of them when she came up.

'I'm hungry. Why don't you take me out for something to eat when your shift is over?' she blurted out, knowing how odd it sounded, trying not to make it come out like an order but an invitation.

He turned to her with a surprised look on his face, just as three men came through the front door and stopped, looking the big room over. Link's eyes instantly went to them, observing them over her shoulder. Their heavy coats, hats and muddy boots, said they were trail riders new in town. The bulge under those full-length coats also made it clear all were armed. Link suddenly felt the old feeling that real trouble had just walked through the door. His hand went for a six-gun that wasn't there. He'd always left the big pistol in his hotel room when working, as house rules required. Without thinking he felt for the little .41 caliber derringer hidden under his dress jacket. He'd never told Katie or her father he carried it in case a real emergency came up. Instinctively, he knew this one was.

'I don't think now is the time for us to leave here,' his voice changed to a low, serious tone just above a whisper.

'What?' She raised hers at being so brusquely rejected, until turning to follow his steady stare at the trio by the front door, surveying the room. 'What is it, Link? Who are those men?'

'I don't know them, but I've known men like them. Get back, Katie. There could be trouble. You stay out of it. I'll handle it.'

'But Link . . .' he pushed her back before starting through empty tables toward the front door. As he came up, the three turned their attention to him.

'You gentlemen looking for some early morning gambling?' Link's voice was steady, his eyes going from man to

144

man, sizing them up, until the biggest one, wearing a wooly, buffalo-hide coat and dirty hat, answered back.

'What's it to you? You the doorman or somethin'?'

'No, I'm paid to keep the peace in here. If any of you are packing hardware, you'll have to turn it in over at the counter.' He pointed toward the check room. 'We don't allow any kind of weapons in the Keystone.'

'You don't, huh? I suppose you serve sarsaparilla to the men instead of whiskey, and perfume them up so they all smell real nice, too?' Mook Bullock's two pals laughed under their breath at his comment. Mook always was good with words and insults.

Link ignored him. 'That's the rules. Empty out, or turn around and leave.'

'Well, what's goin' to happen if we don't want to? We've had a long ride through snow and sleet. We need a drink to loosen up and warm up.' Bullock stood a head taller than Link, growing more irritated at Bonner's insistence. 'You think you can stop all three of us with that popinjay outfit you're wearin'?'

'Yeah, I will. But I'll put the first two bullets in you, stomach high,' Link parted his jacket showing the holstered little derringer.

'Why that pea shooter wouldn't stop a bird!' Mook smiled back, revealing a mouth full of yellowed teeth.

'It'll go deep enough to give you a stomach ache you won't get over. Either get rid of your weapons, or turn around and get out of here. I'm not going to explain it to you again.'

Bullock stared back hard with narrowing eyes. His mouth quivered, weighing the emotion of sudden gunplay. Bonner did not blink. Instead he pulled his jacket fully open to get at the derringer. Mook finally straightened up, a sinister smile creasing his heavily-whiskered face.

'You think you're a real hard case, do yah? Well just maybe we'll see about that even if it's not right here tonight. We'll be back to finish this little conversation. You got a name, hard case? We'd want to know what to put on your headboard.'

'It's Bonner, Link Bonner. Remember what I said. You come back here, you better be clean, or I'll stop you at the door.'

'Don't you worry none. I won't be forgettin' about you. No siree I won't.' Mook turned around, motioning his two pals to follow him out, slamming the door behind him.

Katie rushed across the room to Link. A questioning look played across her face. 'What was that all about?'

'Those three weren't here to gamble, except maybe with their lives. They rode in from out of town. They're not local. From the look of them they're sizing up the Keystone, how many were in it, and how it was laid out.'

'Sizing us up?'

'Yes. To rob the tables and anyone else in here late at night like this when we're nearly empty. They also wanted to see if we had any protection. They found out I was it, not two or three house guards like some places have. They'll be back, Katie. You can count on it. When they do, they'll bring big trouble in with them, unless I can stop them before they start.'

'But if you're right, what kind of a chance do you stand against three men?'

'I've gone up against three men before. I just never told you or your dad about it. This little pocket derringer won't stop them. I'll have to start wearing my six-gun again. I'll try to keep it under a longer coat, so it doesn't show, but

146

it's going back on.'

Katie's face dropped in amazement and confusion, stunned at his frank admission. 'Why didn't you tell us all this before?'

'Because you and your dad wouldn't have hired me, and I needed this job. Now that you know it, you ought to be glad I know how to handle men like that. It's only a matter of time before they come back and make their move. When they do, I'll be here to stop them.'

'Wait a minute, Link. We can hire more help, get some armed guards in here. It's insane to think you can go up against three of them like that.'

'They won't show if the Keystone is armed to the teeth. They'll try something else like robbing players outside, or getting the cash when we transfer it to the bank. The Keystone name is known a thousand miles away from here. Everyone who's heard of it knows it's the big money game. The only way to finish those three off is to let them think they can come back in here and take us down. That way I can end it once and for all. When the word gets out, anyone else with the same idea will think twice before trying the same thing. That's how you handle men like that, Katie. I know their kind. I've had plenty of experience with them. You'll have to trust me that I'm right. I'll talk to your father about this and explain the whole thing to him, too.'

Katie pulled up a chair and sat down, her head spinning. It was almost too much to try to understand. She wondered what kind of man Link really was that he thought so little about facing possible death. She took in a deep breath, trying to compose herself before looking up with a question.

'You make all this sound like it's just an every day job

going to work. Don't you have any fear about yourself, no matter how good you say you are?'

'Most of me died back in Sacramento. I won't explain why. It's something personal I won't talk about. I will tell you I thought coming all this way to Denver might change that. I guess I was wrong. I've had a gun in my hand since I was a kid, and that's the way my life has always been. If I wasn't good at it, I'd been dead and buried a long time ago. Some men are born to be farmers, cattlemen, or maybe go into business of some kind like your dad. I was born to a six-gun and the ability to not hesitate to use it. It's just that simple, Katie. If there's really a God up in heaven, that's what he meant for me to be.'

'No God would do that!'

'Something or someone did.'

'Will you listen to me? Denver has a sheriff, and he can deputize more men to come in here and help protect us. Why do you insist on pitting yourself against three men? That's insane. It's almost like you're. . . asking to die!'

'I've already told you why. Just remember this. That bunch will show up late like they did tonight. The tables will be fat with cash. I'll try to take them at the door before they get inside and can shoot up the place. Players might catch a bullet if they get this far. Keep your eyes on me each night from now on. I'll stay close to the door. When they show up, get anyone still in here down under the tables, and that includes you too. Understand me?'

She rested her head in both hands, slowly shaking it while talking at a whisper. 'I can't believe any of this is actually happening. Why can't you listen to reason?'

If Link's plan met with confusion and resistance from

148

Katie, her father was an even greater challenge. Link carefully explained the confrontation to him and how the trio would return. But Kurt Keystone had always prided himself on running the most widely-respectable gambling establishment in Denver, and the thought of actual gunplay inside the club was abhorrent to him. He questioned Bonner on how he could be so certain the three men would return. No one had ever attempted to hold up the Keystone, and he couldn't imagine three scruffy, trail riders walking through the door, being successful at it either.

'This story of yours is awful hard to believe, Link,' he commented. 'These men you're talking about might only be looking for a chance to gamble a little and have something to drink, even if they are a little rough-looking around the edges. You and I both know how a man can get after a long time in the saddle. They have to blow off some steam. Bright lights, bourbon and women is the way they do it.'

'You'll have to trust me, Kurt. If I'm wrong, nothing will come of it and we can forget about it. But I know how men like that live, and what they're willing to do. These three are hungry wolves just rode out of the mountains. They've lived like animals and think like them too. Because they're in Denver, doesn't change that. Killing to get what they want means nothing. Being in the Keystone doesn't change them either. You have to believe me on this. They'll be back, I can guarantee it.'

Kurt got up from his desk, walking around the big office, pulling at his chin, thinking the whole thing over. He glanced at Bonner. He liked and trusted the man who'd proven to be a big asset to the club, but this wild story was just too much to believe. When he sat back down at his desk, he'd already made up his mind.

'Link, I think Katie's idea to get the sheriff and some extra deputies in here makes more sense to me. I'll talk to John Torrance about it tomorrow. If he will come in and put up a big show, no one in their right mind would try to hold us up. Besides, your idea of taking on three men all by yourself, doesn't make any sense to me either. Why possibly get yourself shot or worse, when the law can handle something like that? I'm a lot more interested in stopping something before it happens, than actually inviting it to start inside my business. I want you to know I do appreciate you telling me all this, and I thank you for keeping your eyes open when you think you see trouble. That's an important part of your job too, and you're good at it.'

Bonner left Keystone's office, convinced Kurt could not understand how serious the threat was. The famous gambling house had been the queen of Denver's establishments for so long, neither Kurt nor his daughter could imagine the real jeopardy it was in. Link realized that the man known as Mook Bullock had gotten a good look at the club and also knew he was the only thing standing between him and his pals taking a fortune in cash both on the tables and from the cash boxes underneath them. Bullock wouldn't hesitate to kill anyone that got in his way. Not for one second.

That night after work, Link walked back to his hotel room. Taking off his jacket, he unbuckled the derringer harness, putting it away in the desk drawer next to the bed. Now it was time to strap on the big six-gun that he'd always felt far more comfortable with. He'd tried to make the Keystones aware of what was coming. They simply could not believe it. The only way you stopped men like

Mook Bullock, Wayne Pardi and Ben Quince was with a flaming six-gun leveled belt high. Bullock would not wait long for his return. Neither would Bonner.

CHAPTER TWELVE

The following two evenings when Link's shift began, he circulated through the usual crowd, greeting customers, keeping an eye on things early on. As the night wore on and the room began to thin out well after midnight, he stayed mostly near to the front door. He was still convinced Bullock and his men would show up late, exactly as they'd done the first time. By the time his shift ended that second night, close to four o'clock, Katie came over with a smug smile on her face.

'Well, those men you were so worried about haven't shown up again, have they? And it looks to me like you've got yourself all worked up for nothing.' She gave his arm a squeeze, consoling him.

'They will. They'll be back, and I hope you're not close by when they do,' he assured her, certain as ever.

'My God, you're so stubborn. Can't you admit you were wrong, just once? You men always think you're so right about everything. Us women are here to show you you're not. By the way, Daddy is having John Torrance in here tomorrow to look things over. I'm sure he's going to use him for a week or so. I thought you'd like to know that.'

'This is your father's place, Katie. He can do what he

wants. I still think it's better if I handle things my way. Not so many guns are involved. That means less people get hurt.'

She stared back at him, slowly shaking her head, her long, red hair cascading down shapely shoulders. 'You know, you never did take me out for something to eat the other night, remember? Why don't we give it a try again this morning? You're almost off shift and so am I. What do you say? It might be better than eating crow, wouldn't it?' She laughed, needling him.

Link abruptly reached out with both hands, grabbing her by the shoulders, turning her completely around. 'Get back across the room, and take everyone with you,' his voice was a short, sharp order.

Before she could protest, she saw Mook Bullock and his two saddle pals push through the front door and stop, looking the room over. A bolt of fear instantly gripped her as Link pushed her away hard, before turning for the entrance. Mook stopped when he saw Bonner coming toward him. He quickly turned, saying something to Pardie and Quince. Both men stepped away, spreading out on either side of him, to not make easy targets.

'Open your coats,' Link ordered, stopping fifteen feet away, squaring off in front of the trio, pulling his jacket back, clearing his own six-gun. 'I want to see you're clean. No weapons.'

All three stiffened at the order, but Mook still had to try to get the last word in. 'You wanna see our long-Johns too, big mouth?'

'Open up or back out that door. I won't tell you a second time.'

'You ain't gonna get that chance ... take 'em boys!' Mook shouted, yanking his long coat open revealing the wicked, sawed-off, double-barrel shotgun he had his hand on.

Bonner knew he had to kill Bullock first to stop that deadly scatter gun. His six-gun cleared the holster before Mook could pull back both hammers on the shotgun. Two thundering shots sent Bullock staggering backwards, falling through the door, rolling out into the muddy street. Pardie and Quince were stunned at the sudden death of their leader, hesitating a fraction of a second before yanking their pistols. Link swung on Pardie next, both men firing almost at the same instant. Pardie buckled to bullet hits in his stomach, as Quince ducked right, firing back wildly as fast as he could pull the trigger. Link felt hot lead cutting into his body. His legs buckled, sinking him to his knees. Quince turned to run, but not fast enough. Link fired his last two shots as he ran out the door, collapsing him into the street. He lifted his head once, trying to crawl a few feet, before dropping face first into the mud. Bonner had backed up his order, but at a deadly cost.

Katie screamed, running wild-eyed across the room to Link, as customers scrambled back up to their feet, shouting for help at the carnage.

'Katie, are you all right? What happened? What's all the shooting about?'

'Daddy, Link's been shot. Get down here, quick!'

Keystone rushed down the stairs two at a time, reaching Katie on her knees, cradling Link's body in her arms. One look was all Kurt needed to know, no doctor was going to help Link. His open jacket and dress shirt were already soaked red with blood from two bullet hits. He was dying in front of their eyes. Link slowly reached up, pulling Katie lower, trying to say something, barely above a whisper.

'Listen . . . to me . . . write . . . James Tate . . . in Mountain Gate. Tell him to . . . come . . . take me home.'

'Take you home, what do you mean? We're getting a doctor in here right now to take care of you. Don't talk like that.' Tears welled up in her eyes, running down her face. Kurt leaned lower, whispering something in her ear.

'No, he's not, Daddy! We've got to get him help. Why isn't someone going for a doctor? Hurry!' Her voice was frantic, shoving Kurt away.

Link tried to say something through a gargled cough. She leaned back down, staring into his eyes, caressing his face with her hand. 'I can hear you. What is it, Link?'

'I . . . told you . . . they'd be . . . back, didn't I?'

'Yes, you did. You were right all along. We should have gotten help. Why in God's name didn't we?' Her shoulders shook with uninhibited sobbing.

Link's hand still held his six-gun. Now it began to relax. He closed his eyes, trying to say something else one last time. He couldn't. His body relaxed as the last vestige of life drained out of him. Link Bonner was dead in her arms. Katie wailed uncontrollably as Kurt tried to pull her away. Instead, she wrapped both arms around Link, refusing to let go, her head buried in his blood-stained shirt.

'Someone get over here,' Kurt turned, looking around the room at the few remaining gamblers standing wide-eyed in fear. 'Get Link off this floor, up onto one of the tables, and cover him up. I don't want anyone else to see him like this. He was a man to respect. He deserves no less, now. I'm closing the Keystone down until further notice.'

Kurt finally pried Katie loose from Link's body. Crossing the room, he started up the stairs, holding her close. Once inside his office, he laid her down on a big, leather, padded couch over against one wall, then sat

155

trying to console her.

'I knew from the start you were falling in love with Bonner. You finally found a man you couldn't buffalo and had some respect for. Now this tragedy has happened. I blame myself for not acting fast enough to have avoided it. I should have gotten Torrance in here sooner. I'm so sorry, Katie. I hope you can forgive me. Try to understand that you're young. You'll have a lifetime to find someone else. Everybody does. Your mother and I were lucky. We loved each other from the start. I married her on her sixteenth birthday, God rest her soul. This misery tonight will heal over time, and you have plenty of it ahead of you. Try to understand what I've said. I love you very much and know things will slowly get better. Let's go home, honey. I'm closing down the Keystone for a while. When things quiet down, we'll open back up again, when you feel right about it.'

James Tate received Katie's letter two weeks later, and made the long buggy ride through snowy mountains to Denver. Kurt Keystone had ordered the undertaker to place Link's body in an expensive casket, kept in the back room of his funeral parlor where frigid temperatures of winter would best preserve it. When Tate arrived, after talking briefly to Keystone about the killing shoot out, he went to the parlor where Linden Coop, the owner, asked him if he wanted to see the body.

'I did a real nice job on Mr Bonner, after I cleaned him up and put fresh clothes on him. I'll open the casket so you can see your old friend.'

'No, leave him be. I don't need to see him. Just get me some help loading up this casket in the back of my buggy. I want to get started out of here soon as possible, and get

Link back home where he belongs. What do I owe you for all this?'

'Oh, nothing. Mr Keystone has taken care of everything. He's a very important man here in Denver. He's well respected, as was your friend Mr Bonner.'

'Link Bonner was a whole lot more than that, but I don't have time to explain it to you. Just get me that help so I can start out right quick.'

Tate left Denver with Link's casket roped in back of the buggy. He drove the two-horse team relentlessly, stopping only when exhaustion, hunger and sleep forced him to. He had to fight his way through dangerous snow drifts and plunging temperatures, while long, white curtains of new snow silently fell, piling up on the horses, Tate and the casket in back. Finally, half frozen and with the horses played out, Tate reached Mountain Gate, to the amazement of locals who said he was crazy to try and reach Denver at that time of the year for any reason, least of all the body of Link Bonner. He presided over Link's funeral, spoke his piece, then retired to the High Timber Saloon, reflecting on the amazing life and times of his old boyhood friend, to the crowd of young cowboys gathered around him.

'I only wish to God I'd been in Denver with Link. If I had, that shoot-out in the Keystone would have ended a whole lot different than it did. Link would be sitting here beside me right now telling you boys about the times we both lived through. But there's one thing I want all of you to understand about the man and his times. Without a man like Link Bonner, the west wouldn't be even close to what it is today.'

'What do you mean by that, Bull?' one of the cowboys questioned.

157

'What I mean is that all this land, and I mean all of it, not just here in the mountains, but way down south to the Mexican border, out west across the high sagebrush desert and over the Sierra Mountains all the way to a salty sea, would still be a wild and dangerous place to live. Men like Link made up their own rules and lived by them. He enforced those rules with a fast six-gun, when there was no law-man with a badge for five-hundred miles in any direction. And even half of them worked both sides of the law for their own benefit. Some of the worst criminals wore a badge for a while until they were either shot down, found out, or forced to give them up. Link did kill a number of men, there's no doubt about that. But there wasn't any one of them that didn't need killing.'

'How could any man need killing? How does just one man decide that?' another listener asked.

'Because some of them were the worst butchers imaginable. They'd kill men, women and even children if they got in their way. They had everyone scared stiff of facing them, except a man like Link. Just look around you now today. You've got stagecoaches running the same roads the old pioneer wagons did that first came west, pulled by oxen teams. The old Indian trails are all grown over, lined by telegraph poles with steel wire that can get a message fifty miles in a wink of your eye, when a man even on a fast horse would take three days. Towns are sprouting up all over the west with churches and schools and newspapers. Men like Link cleared out all the vermin so things like this could happen. No one in Mountain Gate today settles anything out in the street with a six-gun. You go get law or maybe a slick-haired lawyer to end up in court. And I'd have to say I had a small hand in it too, back when I was young and me and Link were riding all over the country together. One thing is sure. The clock don't wait for no one. It's always ticking, always moving on to the next day. It took a man of conviction and a fast gun to make those changes for decent people to set down roots and start a new life in a new land. And I know this, too. I never had a better friend than Link Bonner, and never will. Some people around here say Link was nothing more than a gun-toting killer who took the law into his own hands, but I know better. I was personally with him a lot of those times and saw what happened with my own eyes and six-gun. He did what he had to when he knew he was in the right. Even though none of you will ever know him like I did, he made your life better today for what he did when others wouldn't. That's something I don't want any of you to ever forget. Link Bonner was a whole lot more than just a sensational name on the front of some dime novel. When someone a lot smarter than me writes the real history of the old west, Link's name will be right up high in there. He was a one of a kind man, and we're all better off for it. That's the real legend of the man I called friend, and don't none of you ever let anyone else tell you different!'